# THE FAMILY
# WITH TWO
# FRONT DOORS

**Also by Anna Ciddor**

*Runestone*
*Wolfspell*
*Stormriders*
*Night of the Fifth Moon*

# THE FAMILY WITH TWO FRONT DOORS

## ANNA CIDDOR

ALLEN&UNWIN

SYDNEY·MELBOURNE·AUCKLAND·LONDON

First published by Allen & Unwin in 2016

Allen & Unwin – Australia
83 Alexander Street, Crows Nest NSW 2065, Australia
Phone: (61 2) 8425 0100
Email: info@allenandunwin.com
Web: www.allenandunwin.com

Allen & Unwin – UK
Ormond House, 26–27 Boswell Street,
London WC1N 3JZ, UK

A Cataloguing-in-Publication entry is available
from the National Library of Australia
www.trove.nla.gov.au.
A catalogue record for this book is available from the British Library.

ISBN (AUS) 978 1 92526 664 1
ISBN (UK) 978 1 74336 859 6

Teachers' notes available from www.allenandunwin.com

Cover & text design by Sandra Nobes
Cover images by Anna Ciddor and Shutterstock
Set in 10.5 pt Bohemia by Tou-Can Design
This book was printed in Australia in April 2016
by Griffin Press

10 9 8 7 6 5 4 3 2

www.annaciddor.com

MIX
Paper from
responsible sources
FSC® C009448

The paper in this book is FSC® certified.
FSC® promotes environmentally responsible,
socially beneficial and economically viable
management of the world's forests.

# Contents

*This book is based on the true story
of my Nana Nomi's childhood*

## Chapter 1

# The Letter

THERE WERE NINE CHILDREN IN the Rabinovitch family. The oldest, Aaron, was seventeen, but maybe we shouldn't count him because he was married and didn't live at home any more. After Aaron came the eldest daughter, Adina, then Miriam, Shlomo, Esther, Nomi, Yakov, Devorah and, last of all, the baby, Bluma.

The family lived on the second floor of 30 Lubartowska Street, in Lublin, Poland, and they had two front doors, a blue one and a brown one, because they had to rent two apartments to fit them all in.

Papa Rabinovitch was the rabbi for the Prayer House – the shtibel – on the ground floor. Every day before breakfast he went downstairs to pray. And every day after breakfast he worked in his study, reading his books and waiting for people to come to him for advice.

A frantic young father might rush in to ask him what blessing to say for a new baby. Or a housewife might want to know, 'Rabbi, is it all right to eat this chicken with spots on its liver?'

And Papa would ponder, running his fingers through his long beard, and maybe consult one of his books, before he gave an answer.

Aaron and Shlomo were going to be rabbis too, one day. Aaron proudly stroked the fuzz of whiskers growing on his chin and Shlomo, at twelve, was already leading discussions in the shtibel.

But as for Yakov...Yakov would much rather watch the blacksmith, or even help Mama and his sisters around the house, than sit with his tutor learning the Bible.

'Give him time,' said Papa. 'He is only eight.'

But Mama sighed and shook her head. She remembered Aaron and Shlomo when they were eight, standing behind their father, copying all the prayers.

Our story begins on a Thursday morning in early June. Nomi was in the dining room laying the table for breakfast, and Yakov was following behind, putting out the butter knives. Adina, as usual, was being the bossy older sister.

'Don't bang the plates so much, you'll break them,' she warned, and, 'Watch out, you'll burn yourself!' as Yakov reached past the big brass samovar that was humming and bubbling in the middle of the table.

Esther glanced at the clock on the mantelpiece, and tied a napkin around Devorah's neck. Miriam brought in the bowls of herring and boiled potato. Shlomo put down his prayer book and joined the others at the table. Adina set the teapot on top of the samovar to keep warm. Mama carried in the dish of round brown bagels, and everyone gazed at them hungrily. Bluma, in her high chair, banged her fat little hands and called, 'Me! Me! Me!'

But nobody could take even the tiniest nibble till Papa came back from the Prayer House.

And then, suddenly, there he was in the doorway.

'Mama,' he called out. 'I have heard from your brother in Warsaw.'

With a crash, Mama dropped the plate of bagels on the table. 'Yehoshua,' she cried, 'what does he say?'

The children looked at their mother in surprise. Why was she so excited about a message from Uncle Moyshe?

Papa waved a letter in the air. 'He says the matchmaker has chosen well. The Weinberg boy will be a good match.'

Mama let out a shriek, and threw her arms around Adina. 'My first daughter is going to be married!'

Everyone gaped. Adina, at fifteen, was the right age to be married, but none of them had known Papa was speaking to a matchmaker yet.

'What...What's his name?' Adina sputtered out at last. 'What's he like?'

'He is Mordechai Weinberg,' said the Rabbi, 'the oldest son of a good, religious man in Warsaw. The father – long may he live – runs a business, and he has a generous hand for every charity.'

'A-ah,' crooned Mama approvingly.

'Of course, nothing is settled yet,' warned Papa. 'His family still has to inspect the bride...'

'Inspect the bride!' snorted his wife. 'Where else could they find such a lovely girl, such a wonderful cook? A rabbi's daughter at that, with a fine dowry...'

'But what is he like?' Adina asked again.

'Is he old or ugly?' demanded Miriam.

'Is he tall?' asked Esther.

'Questions, questions...' The Rabbi folded up the letter. 'His mother and his aunts are coming on Sunday, God willing. You can ask them yourselves.'

'On Sunday!' gasped Adina.

'On Sunday!' wailed Mama. 'But that's not possible. Today is Thursday. And tomorrow we have to prepare for Shabbes... How can we be ready by Sunday?'

Papa shrugged. 'Just give them a bit of honey cake and a drop of whisky.'

'Honey cake and a drop of whisky!? Are you mad? They will think we are paupers! We need oranges, chocolates, sweets... And who do you think will bake the cake, and clean the salon, and...? Oy, you have no idea.'

'Mama, your salon is already so clean they could eat off the floor. Now, no more talking. Let's wash our hands and eat.' And Papa strode towards the washstand at the side of the room.

## Chapter 2

# The Market

ARE YOU WONDERING WHAT THE Rabinovitch children looked like? Well, they all had dark eyes and brown wavy hair, but that doesn't really tell you much. As they sat around the breakfast table that Thursday morning – girls down one side, boys down the other (with Mama and Papa at either end) – this is how they looked...

Adina was sitting demurely with her eyes cast down (girls were expected to keep quiet at mealtimes), and taking dainty nibbles of her pickled herrings and radishes. Only the bright spots of colour on her cheeks gave her away.

Miriam, on the other hand, was shovelling boiled potatoes into her wide mouth, and every now and then letting out a little squeak as if she was having trouble keeping her words inside. Miriam was a year younger than Adina, but half a head taller, and while Adina's hair flowed in dark, smooth waves, Miriam's hair stood out in a wild, unruly frizz.

Nomi was seated next to Miriam, though perhaps 'seated' isn't the right word, because she kept wriggling backwards and forwards trying to catch glimpses of Adina around her tall, big-boned sister. Nomi was ten years old. Her hair was plaited into two long braids, and every time she leaned forward, the end of one pigtail very nearly dipped into the bowl of oily herrings.

Next to Nomi was four-year-old Devorah. Devorah was kneeling up on her chair, head bent, curls flopping in her eyes, absorbed in spreading butter on her bagel.

On the other side of Devorah sat Esther. Esther, who was a year older than Nomi, should have been keeping an eye on the little ones. But Esther was gazing into space, dreaming about bride dresses. Esther had no idea that baby Bluma was leaning over the side of her high chair tossing soggy, chewed lumps of bagel onto the floor ...

Papa, in his black hat and long black coat, sipped a glass of tea while he discussed a point of law with his sons. Pale, skinny Shlomo bent towards him, earnest and eager, twirling one of the long locks that hung in front of his ears, but Yakov – pink-cheeked, roly-poly Yakov – was amusing himself by kicking Nomi under the table, and whipping his own feet out of the way when she tried to kick back.

He was most disappointed when Mama moved the herring bowl away from Nomi's plaits and took the soggy bagel out of Bluma's paws. (Mama was planning all the things she had to get done before Sunday, but that didn't stop her noticing what was happening around her table.)

At last the meal was over. The Rabbi picked up his napkin and dabbed at his beard. With a roar of enthusiasm, everyone joined in the blessing.

The moment it was over, the questions burst out again.

'Mama, can I help design the bride dress?' (That was Esther, of course.)

'Mama, what questions will they ask Adina?' (That was Nomi.)

'Papa, how old is Mordechai?'

'Papa, when will the wedding be?'

'Papa, can I help with the chuppah this time?' This was Yakov. When Aaron got married, they'd all said Yakov was too young to hold up a pole for the wedding canopy. But now he was eight.

'Children, children!' Mama clapped her hands over her ears. 'No time! We have to get to market. Yakov, you come too. You can help carry.'

Yakov grinned as she handed him a basket.

A moment later, the blue front door flew open and the children poured out.

'Nomi, look at me!' crowed Yakov. He balanced the basket on his head like a bonnet, and almost knocked over his tutor, who was standing on the doorstep.

Nomi and Yakov exploded with laughter, but Adina shooed them down the stairs, scarlet with embarrassment.

'Behave like a rabbi's children,' she hissed. 'Yakov, take that thing off your head and straighten up your cap.'

Mama gave the tutor a regal nod. 'Ah, Reb Feivish. I am sorry, Yakov will not be requiring lessons this morning. He is helping with the shopping.'

At the foot of the stairs was stored the big, battered pram used by every Rabinovitch baby in turn. Bluma was loaded in, and they set off.

'Good morning!' called Zelig the caretaker, as he hastened to open the high wrought-iron gate for them.

The apartment block rose straight up from the pavement, with a pair of double gates set in the middle of its front wall. Behind the gates, a passageway led through the building to the courtyard in the centre.

'Good morning, Zelig,' chorused the children as they filed past him.

Zelig smiled and waved, then clanged the gate shut and went back to sweeping the entranceway.

Lubartowska Street was a wide, busy thoroughfare. Apartment blocks three and four stories high towered on either side, droshkies drawn by horses clattered over the cobblestones, and shops of all varieties and sizes crammed together along the pavements.

The family crossed the road, and Yakov peered into the ironmongery. It was too small to have a window, but through the open door he could see the gleam of saw blades, axes and chisels...

'Ya-a-akov,' sang Nomi.

He flashed her a grin. 'Race you,' he shouted.

He took to his heels, dodging and twisting among the morning shoppers. Past the grain store he pelted, and the printer's, and the boiled-bean shop where customers were queuing for paper cones of hot, salted chickpeas.

'Sorry, sorry,' he gasped, as his basket bumped and caught on people's elbows.

Here and there, archways tunnelled between the shops to reveal the courtyards behind. As he flew past, Yakov caught glimpses of housewives shaking crumbs from tablecloths, a ginger cat tearing at a pile of rubbish, and even an old woman opening a window to empty her chamber pot onto the flagstones below.

Then he reached the market, and skidded to a halt. All around him was an exciting jumble of stalls. There were chickens penned in baskets squawking and flapping, people shouting and haggling, trestle tables groaning under piles of shiny fruit, and wooden barrels giving off enticing smells of sour pickles and salted herrings.

Nomi came panting up behind him, then Mama arrived, pulling out her shopping list. His other sisters followed, crowding around.

But Yakov's eyes darted past them. He wanted to taste and touch everything.

A boy about his own age sauntered past. He had no forelocks hanging in front of his ears, and no fringes showing below his jacket.

Yakov stared, and the boy stared back, pulling a face. 'Yid,' he growled.

'*Goy*,' Yakov retorted promptly.

'Don't be rude, Yakov,' Adina scolded.

'He was rude to me!'

'That's no reason to be rude too.'

'Yes it is,' Yakov muttered. If someone insulted him just because he was Jewish, he was going to stand up for himself, no matter what Adina said.

Mama folded up her shopping list.

'Miriam, you get the chickens,' she said. 'Esther, you and Devorah go choose a pound of sweets. And cookies. You'd better buy cookies too.'

She turned to her oldest daughter.

'Please, Mama,' Adina burst out, 'can I find some ribbon to sew on my blue dress for Sunday?' Her eyes were bright and pleading.

'But who will buy the fish?' asked Mama. 'That is your job.' She looked down at Yakov and Nomi standing together. 'Could you two manage?'

Nomi looked startled, but Yakov threw back his shoulders. 'Yes!' he said.

'Give Esther that basket then. You won't need it. And here's the money.'

Yakov trotted excitedly beside his sister as she pushed the notes carefully to the bottom of her pocket.

'I like Adina getting married,' he declared. 'We get to do the shopping. And we'll have lollies and cookies to eat on Sunday!'

'They're not for us. They're for Adina's visitors,' warned Nomi.

Yakov was disappointed, but the next moment there was something new to catch his attention. They were passing a pork stall and he glanced curiously at a yellowy pig's head and long pale sausages hanging on display. A man was handing out slivers of pink meat. Yakov longed to pop one in his mouth, just to find out what it tasted like, but he knew it wasn't kosher.

At the fish stalls, Yakov stretched on tiptoe to peer over the rim of a huge wooden tub. Six silvery carp swam round and round inside.

'Let's get that one,' he said, pointing at a huge fish with long whiskers.

'It's too big. We won't be able to carry it.'

'*I* will. I'm strong.'

'All right then.'

The fishmonger said something in Polish that Yakov couldn't understand. He glanced sideways at Nomi. At home, everyone spoke in Yiddish, even Lidia, their Polish maid, but Nomi could speak Polish because she helped with the shopping every week.

Sure enough, Nomi replied, and even haggled with the man as he swung the monster carp out of the water and dropped it, flapping, onto the scales.

Yakov watched the man in fascination. He was so different from anyone in the apartment block or the shtibel. He had a shiny, clean-shaven face and huge muscles that rippled under his shirt. He slapped the fish onto a plank and brought a mallet down on its head with a loud *THWACK*. Catching Yakov's eye, the man gave a wink, took up a giant blade, and with one slash pulled out a fistful of guts, dripping with blood. Almost in the same movement, he rolled the carp in newspaper and handed it to Yakov.

'Dzię... dziękuję,' stammered Yakov.

Nomi counted the money into the man's gory fist. '*Proszę*,' she told him.

Hugging the fish to his chest, Yakov tried to walk. Two steps...Three steps...He felt the huge, heavy bundle starting to slip.

'I told you it would be too big,' said Nomi.

'It isn't.'

'Here,' said a woman walking beside them, 'carry it like this.'

She stopped, and lifted the awkward weight onto Yakov's shoulder. Yakov clutched the end of it.

'Thank you,' he panted.

'Look, there are the others,' said Nomi, and she pointed at Mama and Bluma waiting with the two oldest girls.

Bluma's pram was heaped high with shopping – onions, potatoes, beans and barley for Saturday's chulent – and Bluma was perched on top trying to eat a raw, muddy potato.

Esther and Devorah came hurrying up at the same time.

'Look,' said little Devorah, starting to pull open a brown paper package.

'No, don't open it here. You'll drop them all!' wailed Esther. 'Quick, wrap them up again. Look, we're leaving.'

'We got lollies,' Devorah announced. 'Red ones and reen ones.'

'Not reen. *Green*,' Esther said.

'Reen,' insisted Devorah.

The Rabinovitch family set off for home. Mama went in front, pushing the pram. Behind her came Miriam, swinging the feathered chickens by their necks. Next came Esther and Devorah carrying the caramels, chocolates and cookies, and close on their heels, Adina, with a basket of oranges and a neat little packet tied with string.

Last of all, a long way back and almost hidden by the crowds on the pavement, came Nomi and Yakov. They were each holding one end of the fish now, Yakov walking backwards, looking over his shoulder.

'I told you it would be too heavy,' said Nomi.

'No it isn't,' puffed Yakov.

'Come on, you two,' called Adina, turning to look for them. 'You'll be left behind.'

'Let's run!' challenged Yakov, and twisting around, he took off, with the carp bouncing and swinging behind him.

'Wa-a-ait, I'll drop it,' cried Nomi, and, laughing and stumbling, the two of them hurried to catch up.

## Chapter 3

# Beggars' Day

LUNCH WAS OVER. THE BUSTLE of people carrying dirty dishes into the kitchen had come to an end, and Adina, Miriam and Nomi were left alone to do the washing up.

Nomi turned eagerly to her oldest sister. 'Adina, when the visitors come on Sunday, will we all meet them?' she asked.

'That would be a good way to scare them off!' Miriam exclaimed. 'Yakov would probably turn up with a basket on his head or something.'

Adina lifted a bowl out of the washing-up water. 'I think they just want to meet me,' she said.

She handed Nomi the dripping bowl.

Nomi began to wipe it with her dishtowel. 'Are you scared?' she asked.

'I'm scared they'll ask me questions I can't answer,' Adina admitted.

'*You?* I thought you were Miss Know-it-all,' teased Miriam, and ducked as Adina flicked the wet dishmop at her.

'You'll be all right, Adina,' said Nomi.

'And what about the groom?' asked Miriam. 'When do you meet him?'

Adina scraped more soap shavings into the water and swirled them around.

'I won't meet Mordechai till the wedding,' she answered. 'Aaron didn't see Yochevet till they got married. That's the way it is done.'

Nomi stared at her, horrified. 'But you might not like him. He might be mean. Or really old.'

Miriam clattered forks into the washing-up bowl. '*I'm* not going to marry someone I've never met,' she declared. 'This is the 1920s!'

'Girls!' The three of them jumped as Mama came back into the kitchen. 'You haven't finished the washing up yet!? It's time to get ready. Nomi, go take that bowl to Papa and ask him for coins.'

Nomi hung up her dishtowel and hurried out of the room. She had to cross into the other apartment now, the one where her parents slept. It had an elegant salon for visitors, a study for Papa, and a waiting room for the people who came to see him. But when she reached the connecting door she hesitated. The room she stood in was cheerful and friendly, the linoleum on the floor worn through from countless feet running in and out, and the yellow wall-paint scuffed and chipped. On the other side of the door there was a dark, formal entrance hall with thick floral carpet on the floor and wooden panels around the walls, and Itsek, her father's secretary, lurking in a shadowy corner.

Taking a deep breath, Nomi opened the door and stepped through.

'Ah, Nomi.' Itsek unfolded from his chair — a praying mantis with thin, wavering fingers, long limbs, and stooped shoulders. He fumbled in his pocket, pulled out a few groshen, and tinkled them into the bowl Nomi was holding. 'Your father should be free in a minute,' he said.

Thursday was Beggars' Day. After lunch, all the beggars in the neighbourhood visited every Jewish home, knowing they would be welcomed in and given a coin or a bite to eat. In a few minutes, the brown front door would be thrown open, and Nomi, Adina, Miriam and Mama would be standing ready with a bowl of groshen and a tray of food. (Yakov, much to his indignation, had been sent back to his lessons, Shlomo was down in the shtibel, and Esther, as usual, was minding the little ones.)

A gentleman came backing out of Papa's study.

'Thank you, Rabbi,' he said. He turned and saw Nomi. 'Who have we here?' he exclaimed. 'This must be one of your daughters.'

Papa, who had followed him to the door, nodded and smiled. 'Yes, this is Nomi,' he answered.

'Ach, may she bring you much joy,' boomed the stranger, and left.

'Come in, Nomi. Let's see what I've got,' said Papa.

Shyly, Nomi followed him into the study. This room, with its strange scent of old books, was the only part of the house that she and her sisters didn't help to clean, because Itsek looked after it.

In the middle stood Papa's desk, and the huge leather armchair with the brass buttons. There were treasures hidden inside that desk. Once, Papa had taken a stick of sealing wax from a drawer and melted a drop onto an envelope so that Nomi could press the seal into it. Another time he had let her lick a leaf of gummed paper and miraculously make it sticky. But today, all that he pulled from it was the leather coin pouch. Nomi held out her bowl and Papa poured in a little stream of groshen.

Mama, Miriam and Adina were waiting in the

entrance hall. Mama took the coins, and Nomi stood next to Adina, who was holding a tray heaped high with kugel, Mama's famous noodle pudding.

The two older girls were dressed in grown-up, fashionable dresses, cut short enough to reveal their ankles (modestly covered by thick cotton stockings). Mama, as usual, wore a frilled jabot at her neck (a style that was fashionable when she married), and a dress that swept the floor. Nomi, like any other ten-year-old girl, wore a knee-length dark blue dress with a sailor collar, and her hair twisted into two long braids.

'Open the door, Itsek,' commanded Mama.

The door swung back to reveal the first two beggars waiting on the doorstep.

'Welcome,' Mama greeted them. She gave a gracious bow as old blind Laizer, led by his daughter Hannah, stumbled over the threshold.

Mama glanced expectantly at her daughters.

'Good afternoon,' said Adina, in the special tone of voice she used for visitors.

'Good afternoon,' said Miriam.

'Good afternoon,' whispered Nomi. She managed to smile at Hannah, but Laizer's sightless, upturned eyes made her uneasy.

'Miriam, give Reb Laizer two groshen,' instructed Mama.

Nomi moved close to Adina as the blind man edged forward, a wavering hand outstretched.

'Where's the food?' cried two little boys, bursting into the room.

Fishel and Getzel were cheeky and mischievous, and not much older than Devorah. They made a rush for Adina and tried to snatch at the tray, but Adina lifted it out of their reach.

'Mind your manners,' she scolded. 'Wait for Nomi to serve you.'

Nomi selected two thick slices of kugel, plump with raisins and greasy with chicken fat, and watched with satisfaction as the two little urchins wolfed them down.

'More,' they pleaded.

'You've had your share,' said Adina, but Nomi slipped them each an extra slice, and grinned as they trotted off, looking comical in their cast-off men's clothes, with sleeves and pants cut short, and the waists bunched up with bits of string.

All afternoon the beggars came and went. There was mad old Yenta, who mumbled to herself, and Moishe the Mouth who never spoke at all but always had his mouth gaping in a wide grin. There was Little Nussyn (who kept growing so fast that his wrists and ankles stuck out of his clothes), and Big Nussyn (who was now grown so old and bent that he looked small). There was weary, grey-faced Raisel who lived in one tiny room in their basement with her four children and an ailing husband, and…oh, so many, many more.

Slowly, the huge mountain of kugel on the tray grew smaller and smaller, till at last there was nothing left but crumbs.

'Mama, the food's all finished,' said Adina.

Mama looked down at her bowl. 'And there's only one more coin,' she said. 'Itsek, you had better shut the door.'

'Phew,' Miriam exclaimed, and dropped onto one of the hard wooden chairs that stood against the wall.

Just as she spoke, they heard the *clump clop clump clop* of someone mounting the stairs. Lopsided Wulf, who had lost a leg in the war, peered into the room.

'Am I too late?' he asked.

'Of course not,' said Mama. 'Nomi, run fetch this gentleman an apple.'

When Nomi came back, Wulf was propped on his crutch in the middle of the hall. Nomi held the fruit tentatively towards him.

'Drop it in my pocket,' he instructed.

Blushing, Nomi slipped the apple into the big, loose pocket, which already seemed to be bulging with food.

'Bless you, little girl,' said Wulf. 'May you live till one hundred and twenty.'

He swung himself out of the room again, and Itsek quickly closed the door.

Beggars' Day was over for another week.

## Chapter 4

# Gefilte Fish

'CAN I COOK THE FISH today?' Nomi ran to the kitchen table as Adina picked up the fish knife and began to slice the carp.

'Don't...be silly,' puffed Adina, struggling to cut through the huge backbone. 'You know that's my job.'

'Someone else will have to do it when you get married,' retorted Nomi. She turned to her mother. 'Mama, who will make the gefilte fish when Adina gets married?'

'Miriam, of course,' answered Mama. 'She is the next oldest.' She turned on the tap and began to scrub vegetables. 'Is six carrots enough?' she muttered to herself. 'No ... better I put in a few more.'

Nomi thought of Miriam down in the courtyard surrounded by a cloud of feathers. 'But Mama,' she said, 'Miriam has to pluck the chickens. I can't do that. My fingers aren't strong enough.'

Her mother slapped a carrot onto the chopping board and began to slice it.

'Esther, then,' she said.

'But ...'

Nomi felt a warning nudge from Adina and closed her mouth. Little girls were not supposed to argue with their mothers.

'Esther looks after Bluma and Devorah,' she hissed at her oldest sister. 'I don't have the patience for that.'

'Nomi.' Mama stopped chopping and eyed her younger daughter consideringly. 'You really think you could make gefilte fish?' she asked.

Nomi's heart gave a leap. 'I've watched Adina do it lots of times,' she said.

'So – then maybe you should try,' said Mama.

The next moment, to Nomi's astonishment, she was wrapped in a long white apron that came right down to her toes, and placed in front of the carp.

'Here,' declared her big sister, 'like this.' With a quick twist of the wrist, Adina chopped the flesh out of the first slice and dropped it in a bowl. 'See?' She handed Nomi the small, pointed knife and waited.

Nomi stared at the grey skin lying in a neat, undamaged oval, the glistening white backbone still in place, and felt a surge of panic.

'Come on, there's no time to waste!' exclaimed Adina.

Friday was the busiest day of the week. The fish had to be minced and stuffed, the chulent made, the chickens prepared, the challahs baked, the whole house tidied, the table set, and every member of the family washed and dressed in their best – all before the sun set and Shabbes began.

Very carefully, with the tip of the knife, Nomi began to scrape at the next slice. She had to get the flesh out – like Adina had – without messing up the skin or the bone...

'You don't need to stick your nose right inside it,' scoffed Adina.

Nomi felt her cheeks flush with embarrassment, but she didn't say anything.

Her sister gave an exaggerated sigh. 'I'll be changing the beds,' she said. 'Call me if you need me.'

Nomi worked on in silence while Mama muttered and bustled about, cutting more vegetables for the chulent, checking the dough for the challah, and beating flour and eggs to make noodles for the chicken soup. It was a cosy, peaceful feeling, just the two of them working together.

Then the back door opened and Old Chaim came struggling inside with a basket of coal. Chaim lived in the basement and earned a few groshen doing odd jobs like bringing the family's coal up the back stairs or cleaning their kerosene lamps. As he crashed the basket on the floor, there was a shout from the dining room and Lidia, the Rabinovitches' maid, came hurrying in, waving her feather duster.

'You old fool,' she exclaimed. 'You've spilled coal all over my clean floor.'

'Sorry,' panted Chaim.

He tried to pick up the scattered black lumps, but Lidia brushed him aside, and bent her stout body to snatch them up herself.

Shrugging, the old man hobbled over to Nomi.

'Don't tell me my little Nomi is making the gefilte fish!' he exclaimed.

Nomi beamed at him proudly. She dropped the first pieces of fish into the mincer, wiped her hands on her apron, and began to turn the handle.

'Look!'

They both watched with awe as worms of minced fish oozed out the holes.

'Careful not to mince your fingers,' called Adina. She must have heard the squeak of the mincer all the way from the bedrooms. The next moment, she popped up, peering over Nomi's shoulder. Then, sprinkling flour on the table next to the mincer, she slapped down the lump of noodle dough and began to roll it flat. 'You have to add the onion and bread now,' she reminded her sister.

Nomi pulled a face. She hated cutting onions. They made her cry.

Miriam burst through the back door and dumped the plucked chickens on the koshering board.

'You soaked them already?' asked Mama.

'Yes, Mama. I had to give a hand to Baila Fishman. She's getting too old and shaky to pull out feathers herself. I soaked these while I was helping her.'

Lidia began to chop the chicken, the heavy meat cleaver clanging on the board. Chaim clattered coal into the iron stove, Adina attacked her dough with the squeaky rolling pin, Mama rattled barley into her chulent pot. The kitchen filled with noise and excitement.

Nomi picked up an onion and managed to slash it in two quick chops the way Adina did. Her eyes smarted, but as she raised her hand to wipe them, she stopped, surprised by the feeling of satisfaction that sprang up inside her. These tears were a sign – a proof – that she was making gefilte fish.

Grinning, she threw the onion and a few slices

of bread into the mincer, and leaned her weight on the handle.

Next for the eggs. She chose a small brown one and tapped it sharply against the edge of a glass. With a satisfying *crunch* it slithered out of its shell. Nomi checked anxiously. Only a few specks of shell, and no blood. Adding it to the bowl of mince, she picked up another one.

'Did you check for blood spots?' asked Adina.

'Of course.'

Adina coiled the thin sheet of noodle dough and began slicing it into strips.

Lidia hefted up the heavily laden cutting board, and carried the chicken to the koshering trough under the window. The wooden board had slats in it so the blood could drain into the trough, and Miriam sprinkled on the special flakes of koshering salt, checking to make sure each piece of chicken was evenly covered.

'Salt!' gasped Nomi. She had nearly forgotten to season the fish.

She threw on salt, sugar, and a dash of pepper, then peered worriedly at the black dots in the mixture. Was that enough? Papa liked it peppery.

'Adina,' she burst out, 'how do I know how much?'

'Just put in a bit for now,' said her sister. 'You can always add more while it's cooking.'

Relieved, Nomi set down the pepper mill and picked up the spoon.

'Nomi, is that fish nearly ready?' called Mama.

'Yes, Mama.'

'You still need to put the stuffing back, and make the sauce,' said Adina, hanging the last noodles to dry on a tea towel over the back of a chair.

'I know, I know.' Nomi began to spoon the stuffing into each ring of grey, scaly skin. It wasn't easy. If she put in too much, or pushed too hard, the slice went out of shape, and she had to drop the spoon and reshape it frantically with her fingers. Her face was growing hot and sticky and a wisp of hair fell into her eyes.

'I'm glad it's you doing that, and not me,' commented Miriam, trudging past with a stack of crockery for the dining room.

Nomi pressed the last bit of stuffing into place, blew out her cheeks, and grabbed another onion to slice.

'I'll get the pan down,' said Adina.

As Nomi dashed to the trough where Mama had left the carrots, the room filled with the delicious aroma of frying onion. Nomi glanced over her shoulder. Adina had put the big cast-iron skillet on the stove and was starting to make the sauce.

'Hey!' Nomi stamped across to her. 'I don't need your help.'

Adina raised her eyebrows and cast down the wooden spoon. 'All right, I'll polish the candlesticks then,' she said.

Nomi tossed the fish head, sliced carrots, a jugful of water and a bay leaf into the pan. Now it was time to cook the fish. From the corner of her eye she saw Adina pull up a chair and unscrew the tin of silver paste.

Nomi placed her hands each side of the fish tray. She needed to carry it to the stove, rest it on her hip the way Adina did, and slide each slice carefully onto the simmering onions.

Bracing her muscles, she tried to lift the tray, but it was too heavy. For an instant, she stood there, feeling helpless.

Adina, humming under her breath, picked up a cloth and began to rub.

Nomi ground her teeth. 'I am not going to ask for help,' she told herself. 'I'll move them somehow.'

Taking the egg lifter off its hook, she slid the wide blade under one of her carefully stuffed cutlets, and with her arm held rigid, turned towards the stove. In two steps, she had laid the fish on top of the sauce.

'There!' she whispered.

Lifting every piece the same way, she got them safely to the pan, then stood back and gazed. Nearly all of them were perfect. She didn't care how much her shoulders ached or her fingers stank of onion. Tonight she would set this dish in front of Papa, and he would cry out in astonishment when he found out who had made it.

She felt Adina's arm wrap around her. 'You're a clever girl,' her big sister exclaimed. 'I didn't believe you could make gefilte fish all by yourself, but you did.'

## Chapter 5

# Mama's Wig

YAKOV LOOKED UP EAGERLY FROM his books as the door to his room clicked open. Mama was standing there, her face pink and harassed under her scarf.

'I am sorry to interrupt, Reb Feivish,' she said to his tutor, 'but I need Yakov to run an errand for me.'

Yakov leapt from his desk, thrilled to miss his lessons for a second morning in a row. Mama beckoned him out of the room.

'Yakov, I need you to take my Shabbes wig to Toiba to set for tonight,' she said. 'Go fetch it from my room. The box for it is under my bed.' And she hurried back to the kitchen.

Mama had two wigs: one for weekdays and one for Shabbes. (Every religious woman had her real hair cut off when she got married.)

As Yakov scuttled off, he wondered fleetingly why Nomi wasn't taking the wig today, but then he forgot everything in the excitement of his errand. He shoved open the door to the other apartment and pulled a face at the startled Itsek. Giggling, he plunged into the salon, and flailed his way through the semi-darkness (the long velvet curtains were kept drawn so the sunlight wouldn't fade the furniture). At last, with a gleeful whoop, he bounded across the hallway on the other side, and burst into Mama's bedroom.

There was the wig, perched on a shiny wooden head on Mama's dressing table. But beside it was the billowy white ocean of Mama's bed…

Yakov took a flying leap, and landed in the heap of pillows and eiderdowns. He bounced up and down, laughing and wallowing in the softness, until a feather flew past his head. Then he quickly hopped off.

The other delight in Mama's room was her massive oak wardrobe. Yakov crouched in front of it, running his fingers over the carved lions' heads with their gaping jaws. He pretended he wasn't a little boy in an apartment block any more; he was a shepherd in a field, and these lions were real beasts, attacking his sheep. He was fighting them off with his bare hands like David in the Bible story...He...

'Yakov, what on earth are you doing?'

Adina was standing over him with a load of fresh, starched sheets in her arms.

'Uh...' Yakov sprang to his feet. 'Mama asked me to take her wig for her,' he muttered.

'Well you won't find it there.'

Yakov reached under the bed and backed out, dragging the big box. 'You'll have to wear a wig too, when you get married,' he said.

There was no answer. He glanced up. Adina was staring at the wig with a shocked look on her face, as if this was something she hadn't thought of.

'Try it on,' said Yakov. 'See how you look.'

Slowly, Adina laid her bundle on the bed, and lifted the wig off the stand. It was arranged in a round cushion-shape, a style that must have been fashionable when Mama got married nearly twenty years earlier.

'It...won't fit over my hair,' she said.

'Yes it will.'

Adina sat on the stool facing the dressing table and Yakov drew her long, loose locks away from her face.

'Go on,' he said.

Staring into the mirror, his sister lowered the wig onto her head.

Yakov burst out laughing.

'You look just like Mama!' he sputtered.

Adina snatched the wig off and rammed it into the box.

'My wig won't be anything like that one,' she said. 'Now hurry up. Toiba Grynszpan is waiting.'

'You look like Mama, you look like Mama,' chortled Yakov, as he sprinted out of the room.

'And don't dawdle in the street like you usually do,' Adina yelled after him.

Down in the courtyard, Esther was minding Bluma while Devorah screeched and scampered with the neighbours' children.

'Yakov, come and catch,' Devorah whinnied, darting in and out among the lines of flapping washing.

'Can't!' Yakov called back. 'I'm in a hurry.'

Out in Lubartowska Street, he ran past the windows of the Prayer House, where Shlomo was inside, busy showing off. He trotted past the mikve where men with towels over their arms were heading to take their ritual baths before Shabbes, but then his feet slowed. There was the blacksmith hammering a horseshoe in a cascade of burning sparks, and Efroyim's bakery with its scent of fresh, sweet challahs, and Rubin's apple-juice store...

In two bounds, Yakov reached the front of the apple store, dumped the wig box on the ground and hopped on top to see inside.

The tiny shopfront, barely wider than one customer, had a high counter that opened directly onto the footpath. '*Epl-kvas!* Apple cider!' shouted the large hand-painted sign over the window. (In Lubartowska Street signs were written in Yiddish, for people who lived in the Jewish quarter of Lublin read Hebrew letters more easily than Polish.) Yakov's eyes flew to the juicing machine that made such intriguing squelching and grinding noises behind the counter.

But barely had he caught a glimpse of Rubin pushing in chunks of apple, than there came a loud *CRUNCH* and the lid of the wig box gave way.

'Oops!' he squealed, as his feet disappeared inside it.

'What have you done?' demanded a lady customer, pushing past him to the counter.

'Nothing,' carolled Yakov. 'It's only the lid.'

Clambering out, he gathered the battered remains, and set off again for the hairdresser's apartment.

'Oy, what's happened here?' demanded Toiba Grynszpan.

'Er ... I trod on it,' admitted Yakov.

Clicking her tongue, Toiba lifted out the wig.

'Go away and come back in an hour,' she told him.

An hour! Yakov made a dash for the door. A whole hour to explore! Turning into Kowalska Street, he hurried past the cobbler shops with posters of shoes and boots on their shutters, and round the curve in the road. He was heading for the castle that was now a prison. And there it was, a massive menacing shape filling the whole top of the hill.

Yakov paused and stared. His mind thrilled with pictures of gangsters, kidnappers and murderers locked behind those high battlements; he imagined tiny dark cells and men with brutish, angry faces rattling on barred windows. He gave a shiver of delight, then dropped his gaze to look at the streets branching left and right.

Which way should he go now? Not Szeroka Street. That was just another boring street with expensive shops where Mama liked to walk on Shabbes afternoon, looking in the windows.

Podzamce Street? Yakov's face lit with a grin. He'd never been down Podzamce Street. Mama always said that part of town was dirty and unhealthy – she said all the sewage of Lublin emptied into a river there.

Yakov set off, sniffing with interest at the unpleasant odour that hung in the air. There weren't many shops in Podzamce Street. Most of the buildings seemed to be cottages or small, shabby apartment blocks.

A peddler ambled past with a tray around his neck. 'Lovely plums!' he called. 'Very sweet, just like sugar!'

Yakov glanced at the fruit. They were squishy and mouldy. He wondered who on earth would buy them.

The street followed the base of the hill and Yakov could still see the prison. There was a tall, round tower behind the walls. Was that where the guards kept watch?

He turned another corner. The road surface rippled as if the ground underneath was caving in, and the buildings teetered at odd angles. Barelegged, barefoot girls knelt on the cobblestones in the middle of the road, giggling over a game of knucklebones.

A door flew open. 'Rachel,' a woman shouted, 'what are you up to? I sent you to buy the challahs.'

One of the girls scrambled to her feet and hurried off.

The others stared at Yakov.

'What's your name?' the dirtiest demanded. 'Want to see the river?' She darted to the side of the road and nipped into a crack between two cottages. 'Come on,' she called.

Yakov followed, squeezing past brick walls slimy with mould. He could hear the sound of running water ahead.

A window appeared on his right, and when he peeped inside, Yakov saw a tailor pedalling away at a sewing machine. The man had a row of silver pins clenched between his lips and he was hunched over, feeding a piece of cloth through his machine.

'Hey, what are you stopping for?' called the girl.

Yakov stepped out into the sunlight behind the building. The girl squatted on a muddy bank, pointing down at a stream of brown water and dirty white foam gushing and swirling at her feet.

The smell was overpowering. Yakov wanted to clap a hand over his nose, but if this tailor's daughter could stand it, so could he. Yakov Rabinovitch was not going to be outdone by a girl.

He stepped towards her. The mud squelched. A rat scuttled. He took another step.

His foot shot out, and for one heart-stopping moment he thought he was going to slide right down the bank into the river. Somehow, he kept his balance, but a vision flashed through his mind of his mother's face if he came home dripping in sewage.

'I...I'd better go,' he stammered, and turned to flee, running all the way back to Toiba Grynszpan's apartment.

'Enter,' called the hair-styler as he pounded on her door.

Yakov burst in, and gratefully gulped down the scents of hair oil and hot curling irons. Wigs were stacked around the room now, and Toiba Grynszpan peered at him around a coiffeur of blonde curls.

Her forehead wrinkled.

'*Fui*, what is that smell?' she demanded.

'Uh...'

Both their eyes dropped to Yakov's mud-caked shoes.

'Er, sorry.'

Hastily, Yakov backed out the door, scraped his shoes clean, and sauntered in again.

Toiba was arranging Mama's wig in its box. She picked up the lid.

'I fixed this too,' she said, and showed him a paper glued underneath to hold it in place. 'So no more monkey business,' she warned him.

'No, Mrs Grynszpan. Thank you, Mrs Grynszpan.' Yakov took the box, and, cradling it as if it was made from glass, he set off for home.

## Chapter 6

# Braiding the Challahs

'MAMA, MAMA, IS IT TIME to make the challahs yet?'

Nomi, bending to lift the Kiddush cup from its shelf, heard little Devorah calling and scampering along the corridor, and felt a stab of jealousy. Before Devorah had grown big enough, it had been she, Nomi, who had knelt at the kitchen table playing with a spare bit of dough while Mama kneaded and braided the challahs.

Esther, hurrying after Devorah, came to a gasping halt outside the dining room door.

'Bluma…go crawl for a bit,' she panted. She dumped the chubby baby on the floor and blew out her cheeks. 'Phew!' she exclaimed. Then she dragged the ribbon from her tousled hair, and gave her head a shake.

Nomi placed the engraved silver cup at Papa's place, and checked the table. All the dinner plates were ready, each with a shining array of knives and forks and spoons, a stiffly starched napkin, and a fish plate on top (for her gefilte fish), but she still had to put out the bottle of sweet red Kiddush wine, the breadboard for the challahs, the pearl-handled breadknife, the embroidered challah cloth, the silver saltcellar...

From the kitchen came the sound of Mama's voice, telling Devorah to wash her hands.

Esther crossed to the mirror that hung over the carved walnut credenza, and began to re-tie her bow.

Nomi stared at the long white tablecloth. It seemed to be moving. Then she let out a shriek.

'Bluma, no-o-o!' She grabbed hold of the tablecloth just as the baby gave it another tug.

The Kiddush cup toppled with a crash, and a gilt-edged dinner plate started to slide over the edge of the table. Esther dived to catch it, and pushed it back.

'Little monkey,' she exclaimed.

She crouched down to disentangle Bluma's grubby fingers from the cloth, and the baby broke into loud, protesting sobs.

'Time for your nap,' said Esther. 'Come on.' She hoisted her sister up again and carried her out of the room.

Rather shaken, Nomi raised the cup, checked it for dents, and began to move around the table, tugging the cloth straight.

Adina appeared from the kitchen. 'I'll finish that,' she said. 'You go help Mama with the challahs.'

Nomi stared at her. 'But...'

'Mama says if you're going to cook the gefilte fish, you should learn how to do the challahs too,' Adina explained.

In the kitchen, Mama was leaning over the table pummelling a vast mound of dough. Every Thursday evening she mixed enough dough to make eight loaves (two for Friday night, two for Saturday lunch, two for Saturday evening, and two for the beggars who lived in the basement), and during the night Nomi often heard her creep into the kitchen to make sure the dough was keeping warm, and rising as it should.

'Nomi, come and look,' called Devorah. She was kneeling on a chair leaning eagerly forward.

They both watched, fascinated, as Mama flipped the dough, twisted it, and punched it with the heels of her hands – faster and faster.

Nomi felt a quiver in the pit of her stomach.

Kneading was one of the most important parts of making bread. Quickly, she rolled up her sleeves.

But as she reached the table, Mama stopped, and heaved a sigh.

'That's enough,' she declared. 'You are going to help me to braid the challahs.'

Nomi was disappointed. Braiding was easy – after all, she braided her own hair every morning.

'Can I have my dough now?' cried Devorah.

'In a minute,' said Mama.

Nomi rested her hand on Devorah's shoulder and Lidia, the maid, stopped chopping the apples. The only sound in the room was the gentle rattle of the chicken soup simmering on the stove.

Mama began the Hebrew blessing. '*Baruch ata Adonai Eloheinu melech ha'olam...*'

She tore off a lump of dough, and held it up. '*Ha'rei zo challah,*' she finished.

Nomi wrapped her own fingers in a dishcloth to protect them, and bent down to unlatch the hot iron door of the stove. A blast of heat from the flames almost scorched her eyebrows.

Mama tossed in her lump of dough and Nomi slammed the door shut.

'*Now* I can make my bread,' announced Devorah.

'Yes,' said Mama.

'Yes,' said Nomi.

Lidia went back to slicing apples for the compote, and Mama, too, picked up a knife. She divided the dough into portions: eight for the challahs, and a small blob for Devorah.

'I am going to make a cat,' Devorah declared. 'This is his head.' She began to roll a ball, then pinched off a little bit and held it out.

'You want some, Nomi?' she asked.

Nomi smiled, and ruffled her little sister's hair. 'Thank you. I've got my own piece today.'

Nomi looked down with pride. This wasn't for playing with. This was for making a real challah.

'Nomi, you know what to do?' Mama asked.

'Yes,' said Nomi.

She divided her dough in half, then carefully tore each half into three.

'A cat's too hard,' exclaimed Devorah, and scrunched up her dough.

'Why don't you make the same as me?' suggested Nomi. 'Roll a sausage, like this.' She floured the table, took one of her pieces and began to roll. 'That's right. Good girl,' she encouraged her sister.

Nomi made six even lengths, laid them side by side, and pinched the ends together.

Then she stared at them. She was used to braiding with only three strands. How was she supposed to do it with six?

She glanced sideways. Mama had already whipped up one loaf and was starting on another, but now her deft white hands slowed down so Nomi could follow.

Mama picked up an outside strand of dough and crossed it over the others. Nomi did the same.

'Good,' said Mama. 'Now the left-hand one…and *no-o-w*…bring the first one over the top and down the middle…*So!*'

But Mama could never work slowly for long. Her fingers began to speed up and Nomi hesitated.

'Left one now,' Mama prompted.

Miriam strode into the kitchen. She had changed into her pink silk Shabbes dress. Several long strands of coloured beads dangled around her neck, and her frizz of hair was wound in two rough plaits around her head. She pulled on an apron and began to make the kugel, mixing some of the freshly made noodles with raisins and sugar and chicken fat.

Nomi kept her head bent in concentration. Right one across, left one down…left one across, right one down.

Slowly, a sticky, white braid began to appear beneath her fingers.

'It's working!' she cried.

'You thought it wouldn't?' exclaimed Mama.

The Rabbi's voice rumbled in the hall outside.

Nomi froze. Suddenly, she remembered that when

Papa came back from the mikve he always tasted the gefilte fish. As he came into the room, her heart started beating faster.

'Mm,' he said, with an appreciative sniff.

He crossed to the stove to spoon up some of the sauce. 'Smells good,' he commented, 'nice and peppery,' and he took a sip.

Nomi held her breath.

'A-ahh,' sighed Papa, and smacked his lips. 'That Mordechai Weinberg is a lucky groom! Adina makes a perfect gefilte fish.'

Nomi felt a huge grin split her face. She wanted to shout out loud, 'It was *me* who made this fish, Papa!' But of course she couldn't. That wouldn't be seemly. She glanced at Mama. Would her mother say something?

Mama moved to the stove and pushed her husband aside.

'Yehoshua,' she grunted, lifting the heavy fish pan, 'it wasn't Adina who cooked this fish. It was Nomi.'

With swift skill, she transferred the fish to the serving platter to cool, while Nomi looked on with pride.

'No-omi?' Papa's voice wavered in surprise. 'My little Nomi? Well, well, who would have thought it?'

When Papa left the room, Nomi could still feel the place on her head where he had patted her. She was warm and glowing inside. The Rabbi rarely showed affection to his daughters.

'Lidia, take the fish down to the cellar,' said Mama. 'So it will cool in time for dinner.'

Esther came into the kitchen next. She headed for the water boiler on the stove, and began to fill a tin bucket. 'Devorah, it's time for your bath,' she said.

'Look what I made!' Devorah held up a very long, dirty-white worm, but as it swung from her fingers, the end dropped off and fell to the floor. The little baker let out a wail of dismay.

'Don't cry, we can fix it.' Nomi scooped up the broken half and quickly pinched it back on.

'Now off you go, Devorah,' said Mama.

'I want to bake my bread,' wailed Devorah.

'Here.' Esther dropped it on the baking tray. 'Now, come on, you need to get all nice and clean for Shabbes, and put on your pretty dress. Careful, don't burn yourself,' she added. She headed out of the room, with Devorah holding one hand, and the bucket of steaming water in the other.

Mama glanced up anxiously at the clock. The rest of them still needed to have their baths and get dressed.

'Quick, Nomi, finish that loaf, and Miriam, tell Chaim we're nearly ready for him.'

It was Old Chaim's job to carry the tray of challahs down the stairs, across the courtyard and over the road to Efroyim's bakery. Very few housewives bought their challahs ready-made for Shabbes. Instead, they made their own bread and took it to Efroyim to bake in his big oven.

Nomi prodded the last strand of her bread into place, and threw her arms wide.

'There!' she announced. 'How does that look?'

'Like my hair,' commented Miriam, 'a big mess.' Miriam hated her thick mop of hair.

'It doesn't!' Nomi objected, but then she stepped back and saw that her challah really was lopsided and bulging, just like Miriam's plaits.

'I'd better make it again,' she said, disappointed.

'Looks, shmooks,' Miriam sang out as she opened the back door. 'Who cares? It'll taste the same.'

'It is most important what it looks like,' corrected Mama sternly. 'Nomi, go have your bath now. Your challah will be fine when it rises.' With a sharp tap, she cracked an egg into a small glass bowl and began to inspect it for blood spots.

Nomi trailed across the room, turning at every step to check if her bread was rising yet.

'Nomi Rabinovitch,' said Mama, 'if you don't hurry, you will miss out on seeing the loaves again before Chaim takes them to the bakery.'

Nomi let out a squeak and scurried from the kitchen.

## Chapter 7

# Chaim's Disaster

THE RABBI'S FAMILY WERE LUCKY. They had a
toilet (well, a wooden bench with a hole in the middle
and a metal bucket underneath), and a real tap with
cold running water. Most families in the block shared
the stinking communal toilet in the courtyard, and
fetched their water in buckets from the outdoor
pump. In winter, if anyone spilled water on the stairs,
it froze into ice, and made the steps slippery and
dangerous.

However, not even the Rabinovitch family had a
bathroom. Nomi and her sisters washed in a tin bath
in Esther and Nomi's bedroom. All week, the bath

hung on a hook on the wall, but on Fridays, it was taken down and the older girls helped Lidia carry bucket after bucket from the kitchen to fill it up.

When Nomi entered her bedroom now, Devorah was shivering beside the tub, Esther was towelling her dry, and Adina, wearing only a petticoat, was adding coals to the white-tiled stove in the corner of the room. (Though it was summer, Chaim always lit the stove for bathtime.)

Nomi darted around everyone, threw off her clothes, and jumped in.

'Hey!' roared Adina. 'It was my turn.'

'Mama told me to have my bath right now,' said Nomi smugly.

Adina crossed her arms. 'I can't wait to get married so I won't have to share a bath with all you brats,' she growled. 'I'll have my own bath then, like Mama.'

'If you help me wash my hair, I'll be quicker,' Nomi hinted. Then, 'Ouch!' she squeaked, as Adina poured the kerosene over her head and began to rub it in with rough, angry fingers.

But in a few minutes, Nomi, pink and shining, was pulling on her clean dress. She gave her hair a quick wring-out with a towel, tugged a comb through, and plaited two hasty braids. Her hair was still dripping, and smelling faintly of kerosene, as she ran back to the kitchen.

The tray of loaves was still there. As Nomi burst in, Mama whisked away the cloth that covered them, and Nomi let out a gasp. They had puffed up to twice the size. And Mama was right. Though you could tell which was Nomi's, it didn't look as bad now.

'Here I am!' called Chaim, appearing at the back door.

Nomi twisted round excitedly. 'Look, Chaim, I made this one.' She pointed at the slightly lopsided challah.

'My, my!' beamed Chaim.

'I just have to put on the egg wash,' said Mama, and dunked the pastry brush in the glass bowl.

'Can I do that?' asked Nomi.

Mama shook her head. 'It is very, very difficult not to spoil the loaves,' she said. Using swift, delicate strokes, she brushed each challah with beaten egg, taking care not to squash the air out.

'There,' she announced. 'And now...' She untied her apron and flung it over its hook. 'It's time for me to get dressed.'

Mama was gone from the room before Chaim even reached the tray, laden with its eight precious loaves.

As the old man lifted it up, Nomi saw that his arms were trembling; she saw the heavy, awkward burden begin to tilt, and...

'Careful!' she cried.

But it was too late. One of Mama's challahs rolled

over the edge and landed with a soft, soggy thud on the floor.

Chaim crashed the tray down again and gathered up the bread. They both stared in horror. The loaf looked as if it had been run over by a droshky.

The old man began to cry.

'You...You better go tell your mama,' he whimpered, and laid it on the table.

Nomi's chest tightened. Mama would be angry with their old servant. She might even say he was too frail to work for them any more.

Then a daring thought shot through her. Could she fix the challah herself? Maybe Mama need never know.

Snatching up the ruined loaf, she tried to knead it, but the egg wash had made it sticky. It clung to her fingers.

'Chaim, quick!' she squeaked. 'Sprinkle some flour on.'

'Flour?' Chaim looked round in bewilderment.

'*There!*' Nomi jerked her chin at the white enamel shaker on the table.

Nomi let out a breath of relief as the dough grew firmer. Swiftly, she rolled out six fresh strands, and began to braid them. This time she had to make a challah that was perfect, a challah that looked like Mama had made it herself.

'Right one across...left one down...' she chanted. 'Left one across, right one down.'

There were footfalls in the next room. Her heart stopped beating. What if someone came in, and saw what she was doing? But no one did.

The loaf was finished. Quickly, she laid it on the tray beside the others and covered it with the cloth.

'It...it's so small,' stammered Chaim.

'It's got to rise,' Nomi told him, and clenched her fists, praying that it would. 'Wait here. I'll come back soon...Mama will be wondering where I am...' and she flew towards the door.

'But they've got to be baked,' cried Chaim. 'And it's getting late.'

'I know, I know...'

In the dining room, Nomi caught a glimpse of Bluma and Devorah propped on the sofa with their legs stuck out, like two frilly dolls. Esther sat between them, drawing pictures. Adina was there too, with a feather duster in her hand.

'Nomi!' called Adina. 'Check Yakov has washed properly. He came home all spattered in mud. And you need to do your hair again,' she added in a yell. 'You look like a scruffy tailor's daughter.'

'Yes, Miss Bossy-Boots,' Nomi muttered. Hurtling past the boys' room, she banged on their door. 'Adina says to wash properly,' she called.

As she charged over the threshold into the other apartment, she caught herself up, and tried to walk more sedately.

'Good afternoon, Miss Nomi,' said Itsek.

'Afternoon!' she panted.

She wove her way through the salon, and into the little hallway outside her parents' bedrooms. Still trying to catch her breath, she rapped on Mama's door.

'Is that you, Nomi?' Mama's voice rang out.

'Yes, Mama.'

Every Friday, it was Nomi's special job to help Mama choose what jewellery to wear. Now, when Nomi entered, she saw Mama waiting at her dressing table. Nomi hurried forward as her mother lifted the jewellery bag out of her drawer and plunged her hand inside.

Mama opened her fist, and Nomi gazed with pleasure at the brooch she had pulled out. It was Nomi's favourite – the gold bird with outstretched wings, encrusted all over with sparkling diamonds. Mama brushed off the sawdust that kept it protected inside the bag and pinned it on the lace jabot at her neck.

'Now you,' she said, holding out the linen bag.

Smiling with anticipation, Nomi dipped in her hand and felt around in the sawdust. Her fingers closed on something delicate and spiky and she drew it out. It was the bracelet of golden vine leaves entwined with tiny ruby flowers.

One by one, she and Mama laid the rest of the treasures on the dressing table – the silver filigree brooch, the pair of ruby and diamond earrings, the five different ruby bracelets, the gold chain, the string of pearls...

'So, what else will I wear tonight?' asked Mama at last.

Nomi ran her eyes consideringly over the jewels. As she did so, she caught the faint sound of a cry.

'No-omi!'

Nomi felt the blood drain from her face. It was Chaim, calling her from the kitchen. She had forgotten the challahs!

She snatched up two bracelets at random and shoved them into Mama's hands. Had her mother heard Chaim calling?

Mama held out her wrists so Nomi could do up the fastenings. Nomi fumbled impatiently. Usually, she loved to linger in the room, helping Mama put on jewellery, watching her dab perfume on her temples, and adjust her Shabbes wig. But today...

The clasps snapped shut and Nomi backed towards the doorway.

'I ... I—' she muttered.

Mama stared at her with a startled expression.

'I...' Nomi waved her hands vaguely, then turned and charged out the door.

'Did it rise?' she gasped, bursting into the kitchen.

She flew to the tray of challahs and pulled off the cloth. Yes!

Lidia was in the kitchen too, scrubbing the table, the wooden brush with its yellow bristles swishing ferociously around the tray.

'I can't get this useless old man to take the challahs away,' grumbled Lidia.

'That's because they're not finished. I still have to put on the egg wash,' cried Nomi, looking round frantically for the bowl Mama had left behind. Had Lidia washed it?

'Here,' said Chaim. He was holding it protectively in his hands.

Nomi knelt on a chair, and very, very gently painted the last dregs of egg onto the loaf.

When she laid down the pastry brush, she realised she'd been holding her breath, but her challah was perfect. Just like Mama's.

'All right, Chaim, you can take them now,' she said.

The old man's face was creased with worry.

'I hope it's not too late,' he said.

As he leaned forward for the tray, she wanted to warn him to be careful, but she choked back the words. Of course he would be careful. She saw his arms tremble, but this time the tray didn't tip. Nomi ran across to hold open the back door. Chaim walked towards her with slow, ponderous steps, then out into the narrow, dark passageway. She stood and watched till he turned onto the back stairs.

Now he would be going down … crossing the courtyard … going out into Lubartowska Street, entering the bakery …

Nomi closed the back door, staring, unseeing, at the peeling green paint. Was it too late for all the loaves to be baked and brought back before sunset? What would Papa say if there were no challahs for Shabbes?

She turned into the kitchen again, biting her lip. Please let it not be too late!

## Chapter 8

# Is it too late?

LET'S FIND OUT WHAT YAKOV has been doing all this time. When Nomi knocked on his bedroom door, he was wallowing in a hipbath with his face submerged, pretending to be a whale. A moment later he shot up, spouted a mouthful of water, and slopped half the contents of his bath onto the bedroom rug. You see, while the girls shared one bathtub, the boys shared another.

Shlomo always washed first, scrubbing himself from top to toe without splashing a drop. While Yakov played, he dressed in his Shabbes clothes: an ankle-length kaftan of black satin, just like Papa's (next year, when he was Bar Mitzvah, he would wash at the mikve like Papa, too), a sash around his waist, and a black hat on top of his skullcap. As a final touch, he twisted his damp forelocks into long, perfect curls with his fingers.

'I'm a crocodile now,' roared Yakov. 'Throw me something to eat.'

'No, you might splash me,' said Shlomo, and he sat down at their desk to wait.

Yakov sloshed around till the bathwater grew too cold. When Shlomo refused to fetch a jug of hot water to warm it up, he hopped out and crouched in front of the white-tiled stove, wrapped in a towel.

Now it was Yakov's turn to dress. He put on his starched white shirt, and reached for his pants.

'You forgot your tsitsis,' crowed Shlomo, watching like a hawk.

'I did not,' said Yakov. 'You just didn't give me time to put it on.'

The tsitsis was a rectangle of white cotton with a hole in the middle and fringes tied in tassels at each corner. Every morning, Yakov held the tassels, chanted a Hebrew prayer, and touched the long, dangling threads to his lips. But now he just had to slip the tsitsis over his head, on top of his shirt.

At eight years old, Yakov didn't dress like an adult yet. He wore a short vest and jacket (the fringes showed below the jacket), a pair of knee-length pants, and long black socks. As he put on each item, he let out a sigh. He never liked putting on fresh Shabbes clothes. They were not as soft and comfy as the ones he'd been wearing all week – especially the starched shirt and the hard, shiny shoes.

'And your cap,' said Shlomo, jamming it on his younger brother's head.

When they stepped out of their room, they were almost bowled over by Mama, magnificent in jewels and Shabbes wig, charging along the passageway.

'Where is Chaim?' they heard her shout as she swept into the kitchen. 'Why hasn't he come back with the challahs? Why hasn't he taken the chulent?'

Yakov glanced into the dining room. The long table was ready, with all the crockery, cutlery and glasses set out in a glittering array along the pure white cloth.

Papa strode in from the kitchen bearing two shiny candlesticks. He placed them in the middle of the table, and turned back for more. There were eleven silver candlesticks and four oil lamps to be brought in from the next room.

'Nomi, Yakov, come here,' cried Mama.

Yakov bounced into the kitchen and found Nomi there, looking pale and upset.

'That man is getting too old and unreliable,' railed

Mama. 'You two – take this to the baker...' She dumped the chulent pot in a wicker basket, 'and find out what's happened. Be quick!'

If this pot of raw meat, beans and barley did not reach the baker in time, the Rabinovitch family would have no hot lunch tomorrow. Fires were forbidden on Shabbes and their own small oven would soon be stone cold. But the baker's huge oven stayed warm even when he put the fire out. All through the long night and morning it would keep on cooking. That's why all the housewives sent him their chulents.

Grasping a handle each, Yakov and Nomi dragged the heavy basket off the table and headed for the back door.

'Do you... know... what's happened... to Chaim?' panted Yakov as they heaved it down the steps.

Nomi glanced over her shoulder, then answered in a hoarse whisper.

'He dropped one of the challahs,' she hissed. 'But Mama doesn't know. I braided it again, only it made him late. And now...' Her voice rose to a worried squeak. 'I'm scared the bread won't be ready in time! Or the chulent!'

Yakov was too shocked to speak. In silence, they staggered across the courtyard.

'You're late,' warned Zelig the caretaker, as he opened the gate for them.

'You're late,' called a last black-clad figure hurrying from the mikve.

'You're late,' panted the Widow Brafman, bustling past them with her challahs.

'Come on,' urged Yakov, almost jerking the basket out of Nomi's grasp.

Now there was no one in sight except Peretz the Shammes, the beadle (and gravedigger) from the shtibel, who was rapping on doors and windows and calling out warnings. 'Time to light the candles,' he called. 'Time to light the candles!'

He spied the two children lolloping across the road, and shouted after them.

'You better hurry,' he warned.

A lone figure emerged from the bakery: an old man with a loaded tray in his hands.

'It's Chaim!' gasped Nomi.

A smile creased Chaim's face as Yakov and Nomi crowded close to him, exclaiming at the delicious, fresh-baked scent of the loaves, and the glistening brown crusts.

'They're perrrfect,' purred Nomi. Then she tugged at her side of the basket. 'We have to take the chulent in,' she said. 'Come on, Yakov.'

The baker's shelves were stripped bare, and there was no one in the shop.

'Efroyim!' called Nomi worriedly.

The baker erupted from the door at the back. He was a mountain of a man and the children had to look up over a vast stomach and forest of red whiskers to see his face.

'You're late,' he growled. 'I have already closed the oven.'

'Oh, *please*,' pleaded Yakov.

To his surprise, Nomi threw back her shoulders and spoke in a haughty voice. 'You will please put this one in too,' she announced.

She sounded like Mama.

The giant baker gazed back at her, then a rumbling sound came from his chest.

'Very well,' he replied. 'The Rabbi's family must have their hot lunch.' Reaching over the counter, he plucked the pot out of their basket with one hand. 'Now go on, hurry home. It's candle-lighting time. Good Shabbes.'

'Good Shabbes! Good Shabbes!' the children called, and they scampered out of the shop.

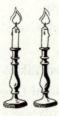

### Chapter 9

# The Sabbath Queen

THE WHOLE FAMILY WAS WAITING, crowded around the candlesticks, when Yakov and Nomi burst back into the dining room.

'Ssh, hurry, quiet!' voices hissed as they scurried forward.

Yakov pushed in next to Shlomo and turned to face Mama, ready with the matchbox in her hand and the white lace scarf draped over her Shabbes wig.

'All right, Devorah,' said Mama.

The four-year-old raised her little fist, and Adina hoisted her up so she could reach the charity tin hanging from the doorframe. With a loud *clinketty clank*, the two coins dropped in, and Devorah slid to the floor again.

At last it was time for the candles. Mama struck a match and leaned forward. Yakov watched in suspense – as he always did – to see how many she could light before the match burnt too low. First came the elegant, tall candlesticks for Papa and Mama, then the smaller ones for the children. The match burnt lower and lower, and Yakov let out a disappointed sigh as Mama dropped it on the metal tray. She picked up Nomi's candle, and used it to light the last few candles, and then the four oil lamps for the little brothers and sisters who had died as babies.

Solemnly, she drew her hands in three circles above the hot, bright flames, covered her eyes, and began to pray. At the sound of the words, Yakov felt Shabbes flow into the room, as warm and real as the heat that poured off the candles.

'*Baruch ata…*'

When the blessing came to an end, Mama kept standing there, her fingers pressed over her eyes, and Yakov knew that now she was offering up her own silent prayer. What was she asking for? A new dress? Some more jewels? Another baby?

At last Mama dropped her arms and smiled. 'Good Shabbes,' she murmured.

'Good Shabbes,' everyone shouted in reply.

'Will Dina have candles too?' demanded Devorah.

'Adina?' asked Mama. 'You mean when she gets married? Of course.'

'Eleven like us?'

'Oh no,' gasped Adina. 'Just two.'

Devorah beamed. 'One for you, and one for Mordechai!' she crowed.

Adina turned scarlet.

Papa proceeded to carry the candles, two by two, into the other rooms. Yakov watched anxiously. When darkness fell, those fragile flames would be their only lights. If one of them went out, no one would be allowed to light it again. But, as usual, Papa delivered them safely.

'Come on, sons,' he called, jauntily leading the way to the front door.

Downstairs, an air of expectation filled the court-yard as men and boys from all directions came hurrying towards the shtibel.

They crammed into the entranceway, shouting greetings, exchanging news, jostling for a turn at the washstand. Yakov was battered by elbows as he scooped up water with the dipper, poured it over his hands, and muttered the blessing. As he wiped his fingers down his jacket, he searched the crowd for his brother Aaron.

There he was!

Yakov squeezed his way into the mob, scrambled under a table, and bobbed up in front of his big, married brother, grinning widely.

'Hello, you cheeky beggar!' exclaimed Aaron. He gave Yakov's sidelock a tweak, and slipped a caramel into his hand.

The shtibel was a big, plain room with bookshelves against whitewashed walls, a wood stove for heating, and a scattering of tables and benches. The congregants sat around the tables, just as if they were eating dinner at home (in fact, the ones who studied all day, like Shlomo, ate their meals there, pushing prayer books out of the way and bringing bits of bread and herring out of their pockets).

The only spot of colour in the room was the Ark, the large cabinet that stood against the eastern wall. It was decorated with pretty embroidered curtains, and inside were stored the Torah scrolls (the first five books of the Bible). A gas lamp made of brass and glowing red glass hung in front.

Papa, the Rabbi, sat on a special seat close to the Ark, and his three sons had places on a bench beside him. As Yakov sat down, Peretz the Shammes bellowed for silence.

The service began, and Yakov copied everyone else, standing when they stood, and bowing towards the

Ark (though not as fervently as Shlomo, who almost whacked his knees with his prayer book).

When everyone else sat down, Yakov did too, gazing out the open door and sucking on his caramel. He could see chalk marks on the flagstones of the courtyard, where girls had been playing hopscotch. He could see the windows of apartments that overlooked the yard, and women and girls moving around inside behind the white lace curtains.

But as the dusk crept in, all the familiar sights began to melt away. The walls around the courtyard turned grey and shapeless, and merged into the dark sky. The water pump and the smelly outhouse vanished in the shadows. Finally, all he could see were glowing patches here and there where candles shone in the windows.

Suddenly, everyone in the Prayer House surged to their feet again, and Yakov leapt up too. Now everyone turned to face the door and burst into song, welcoming the spirit of the Sabbath: the Sabbath Queen.

'*Lecho dodi, come, my beloved...*' they sang at the top of their voices, filling the whole room with song.

Yakov felt goosebumps rise on his arms and hairs prickle on his neck, the way they always did at this moment. He almost expected a real queen to walk in the door.

Fifteen minutes later, the service was over. Rabbi Rabinovitch blessed his congregation, and everyone wished each other 'Good Shabbes, peace be with you', and crowded towards the door.

Aaron pinched his little brother's cheek. 'See you tomorrow,' he said, and hurried away to take Shabbes dinner with his wife's family.

But Papa wasn't ready to leave yet. He halted by the stove, where a couple of strangers were talking with the Shammes. Yakov and Shlomo waited impatiently till Papa, as usual, invited the newcomers home for dinner, then they all crossed the courtyard together – the Rabbi and his sons, Peretz with the two strange men, and Papa's secretary, Itsek.

As they started to climb the stairs, the familiar Friday-night scent of chicken soup came wafting down to them, and Yakov pounded upwards, his stomach growling.

## Chapter 10

# The Strangers

'Here they are!'

Nomi and her sisters scrambled, squealing, to the side of the room as Papa and the men came pouring in.

'Good Shabbes,' bellowed the men, and they launched into song, stamping and clapping around the table.

'*Sha-alom A-aleichem*,' they trumpeted, and then they sang the one about the glory of a wife who was a good housekeeper, and Mama stood up straight and proud, diamonds and rubies sparkling, silk dress shimmering in the candlelight.

Watching from the side of the room, the Rabinovitch girls smiled and clapped (except for Miriam, who was sulking because boys were allowed to sing and girls weren't). But when the music came to an end, they all rushed to Papa.

He blessed his sons and then his daughters, holding his hands above their heads, and Nomi tried to feel calm and holy, but inside she was churning with nerves and excitement. In a few minutes Mama would be serving the gefilte fish, *her* gefilte fish...

Now it was time for the Kiddush. Everyone clustered around the table, and Nomi gazed curiously at the two strangers standing opposite: a tall, clean-shaven man with tanned skin, wearing a three-piece suit, and a shy-looking religious lad, not much older than Aaron. The tall man caught Nomi looking at him, and sent her a grin.

Immediately, Nomi felt a sharp nudge in the ribs.

'Don't be so bold,' muttered Adina.

Nomi coloured, and quickly cast her eyes down, but in a moment she was looking up again.

A hush had fallen in the room, and Papa was filling the goblet to the brim with the ruby-coloured wine. He raised it in the air to begin the Kiddush.

'*Yom hashishi-i-i...*' he chanted.

He drank from the cup, and passed it along for everyone to sip. Nomi saw Yakov tilt his head back for a big gulp, blink rapidly, and struggle not to cough.

The wine had a sweet, fiery taste, but there was not much left by the time it reached the girls. Devorah peered down at the dregs and opened her mouth to protest. Quickly, Nomi pressed a finger to her lips. This was a time for respect and quiet.

The empty cup came back to Papa again. Without speaking, he set it down, and crossed to the washstand. He poured water three times over his hands, dried them carefully, and said the blessing.

Then he turned back to the table, and waited for everyone else to wash their hands in the same way before he lifted the covering off the bread.

Nomi's heart skittered in her chest as she gazed at the two challahs. Across the table, Yakov waggled his eyebrows at her. They both knew if it hadn't been for her, the Rabinovitch family would be having no bread for Shabbes!

Papa lifted the loaves to recite the blessing, and when he set them down again, thirteen voices shouted a grateful 'Amen'. Papa picked up the pearl-handled knife, and thirteen hands reached eagerly for a slice. The next moment, the beautiful shiny brown challahs had been hacked to pieces, dipped in salt, and crammed into hungry mouths. Kiddush was over. Now they could eat.

Mama and the girls hurried to the kitchen.

In here, a table was laid for Shabbes too (it would not be seemly for the Rabbi's wife and daughters to eat in the same room as the visiting men) but first they had to carry the food to the dining room.

'Nomi, come help serve,' ordered Mama, picking up the huge platter of gefilte fish.

When Mama set the platter on the table, Nomi basked with pride as all the men 'Ah-ed' in admiration. The sauce had set perfectly, and the cutlets of fish lay in a lake of glistening jelly, dotted with circles of carrot.

She gave her father the first slice, and watched tensely while he sprinkled it with grated horseradish and took a bite.

He chewed, swallowed, and looked up at her, smiling.

'Perfect,' he said.

Nomi almost waltzed back to the kitchen, where Adina, Miriam, Esther and Devorah were waiting to wrap her in a hug.

'He likes it!' she whooped.

Then Mama came bustling in with the leftover fish.

'Eat, eat!' she ordered.

At last, Nomi could taste her own cooking. She took a bite, and grinned. It was sweet and spicy and juicy – just the way it should be.

Tonight, as on every Friday night, the kitchen was strangely pristine and peaceful. The spatterings of flour and eggshell had been wiped off the floor, there were no more noodles hanging over the backs of chairs, and no more cuts of raw chicken dripping in the draining trough. The table was covered by a white damask cloth and laid with gold-edged plates.

In the next room, the men began to sing again.

'Time for the next course,' announced Mrs Rabinovitch.

The soup bowls were lined up ready by the stove with the noodles inside them. Mama clattered the lid off the saucepan and began to ladle out the steaming chicken broth.

Gingerly, Nomi picked up one of the bowls, trying not to scald her fingers, and followed her sisters into the dining room.

Miriam served the Rabbi (after all, she was the one who made the soup), and Nomi shyly slid her bowl in front of the dark-faced stranger. He grinned again, his teeth white and startling against his brown, weathered skin.

Nomi realised that Miriam was staring at him too. They knew he had to be Jewish, for Papa had met him in the shtibel, but he looked so strange...so different from the other men they knew. Clearly, he spent his days in the sunshine, not sitting indoors poring over books.

Back in the kitchen, the girls gulped down their

soup as fast as they could, then leapt up to peer round the door at the men.

Papa was talking to the dark-faced stranger. 'Reb Hirsh, tell us about the Land of Israel,' he said, and turned to his sons. 'Shlomo, Yakov, did you hear – this gentleman lives in the Holy Land!'

The two boys gaped.

'Are there really deserts and camels and palm trees there?' Yakov blurted. 'Like the pictures in books?'

Reb Hirsh chuckled. 'Of course,' he replied. 'I have even ridden on camels—'

Nomi watched Yakov's eyes grow wider and wider as the man talked. She knew her little brother was imagining himself wandering in a desert, like Moses in the Bible.

'Girls, I need your help,' called Mama.

The sisters spun round and rushed to pick up the platters of chicken and vegetables and carry them into the dining room.

'Potatoes!' exclaimed the dark-faced man as Nomi leaned over to serve him. He rubbed his hands. 'Mmm, the other week, I tried to buy potatoes at the market in Jerusalem. But the shopkeeper cheated me. Do you know what I found in the bag when I got home? Nothing but oranges.'

Everyone in the room stared at him in astonishment, and he let out a guffaw of laughter, slapping his hands on the table.

'Oh ho ho,' he roared, and wiped his eyes. 'In Israel, oranges are cheap, you see. And so are grapefruit, and lemons. Those we can feast on to our heart's desire. But potatoes – we rarely get potatoes. Or apples,' he added, glancing at the bowl of apples and nuts displayed on the credenza.

With that astounding remark, Reb Hirsh tucked into his potatoes, and Papa turned to the other stranger, the one wearing the black hat and long black coat.

'So, Reuvi,' he said, 'you study at the Mesivta Yeshiva in Warsaw ...'

'Yes,' the boy muttered. He looked embarrassed at becoming the centre of attention.

'Do you know a boy called Weinberg?' Papa persisted.

'Mordechai? Of course! He is a bit younger than I am but he is very clever. And his father is a great supporter of our yeshiva.'

'Ah, yes, Reb Weinberg is a charitable man, I am told. He owns a factory ... saucepans, or something ...'

'Yes, sir, enamel cooking pots. They are sold all over Poland.'

Papa stroked his beard. 'And Mordechai ... he is a good student?'

'Oh yes, sir. One of the best. He could be a rabbi

one day, but I expect his father will want him to work in the business.'

Excitedly, Nomi swung round to see her big sister's face. To her astonishment, instead of beaming with pride, Adina was looking worried. Nomi stared at her. Why wasn't she proud to have a fine scholar for a husband? Then, with a stab of shock, she understood. If Mordechai joined his father's business, Adina would have to move to Warsaw. Nomi felt a sinking, frightened feeling in her stomach.

## Chapter 11

# Shabbes

YAKOV AND SHLOMO SCURRIED AS fast as
they dared towards Efroyim's bakery. Running was
forbidden on Shabbes, but breakfast on Saturdays was
barely enough to feed an earwig, and after the long
morning of prayers even Shlomo was eager for lunch.

'Let the Rabbi's children through!' called Efroyim,
and obliging hands pushed the two boys to the front.

'Ah!' cried Mama, when Yakov and Shlomo
returned, panting, to the apartment.

She heaved the pot of chulent out of the basket,
and placed it on the kitchen table. Then she inspected
the dough ring around the lid. Yakov held his breath.

If steam from any other chulent could have seeped inside, Mama would not let her family eat it. She always worried that other chulents in the oven might not be kosher. Once, she had spotted a neighbour using a meat cleaver to cut her cheese, and it was not kosher to mix meat and milk...

But today she straightened and nodded. Yakov and Shlomo heaved sighs of relief. The seal was not broken.

'Lunch is ready!' their mother announced, and they followed her into the dining room.

Yakov took a place beside Aaron, grinning up at his big brother. For Yakov, the best part of Shabbes was having Aaron at home for a few hours.

Papa began the Kiddush, and Yakov gazed over the spread on the table: cold fried herrings and potatoes, gherkins and sauerkraut, a salad of raw onion and boiled eggs, gefilte fish and horseradish. And this was only the first course! In the kitchen a hot, steaming chulent was waiting, and baby carrots in glistening honey glaze, and leftover kugel...

Finally, it was time to sit down and eat. For a few moments the only sounds were munchings and murmurings, and occasional giggles from Yochevet, Aaron's wife, who had dimpled cheeks, dark, dancing eyes, and a perpetual giggle.

Then Shlomo broke out in an excited voice.

'Papa, I saw Reb Hirsh smoking this morning!'

Yakov glanced sideways at Aaron. His older brother raised one eyebrow. Somehow, Shlomo always found something to be righteous about.

'He was lighting a fire and breaking the Shabbes,' Shlomo persisted. 'That's wrong, isn't it?'

'Yes, Shlomo,' the Rabbi replied, 'of course that is wrong.'

'Then why did nobody say anything?'

Papa helped himself to more chulent.

'Shlomo,' he said, 'Reb Hirsh shaves his face, he wears ordinary clothes … He is not so religious.'

'But Papa, if one of us lit a fire on Shabbes, the whole community would scream at us. Why is it worse if *we* do something wrong?'

'Because a stain on a silk coat shows up more clearly than a stain on ordinary cloth. Now, eat your lunch.'

When the meal was done, Papa patted his stomach, hoisted himself up, and ambled off to his room to digest his food. Mama collapsed for an exhausted sleep on her big feather bed. The girls piled up the dirty dishes and carried them off to the kitchen (though they couldn't wash up till Shabbes was over), and Itsek the secretary disappeared to his shadowy corner in the entrance hall.

The three Rabinovitch boys plumped down on the sofa.

'Who's ticklish?' demanded Aaron, and the next moment the three of them were screaming and rolling around with laughter.

'Stop, stop!' gasped Shlomo, clutching his sides. 'I'm going to be sick.'

'All right, it's guessing time then.' Leaping to his feet, Aaron poked his head forward, fumbled with an imaginary pair of spectacles, and began a long-legged, spidery walk.

'You're Itsek!' crowed his younger brothers.

'My turn now,' squawked Yakov, jumping off the sofa.

He glanced round to check they were alone, then gave his head a regal toss. 'Yakov,' he said in a squeaky, haughty voice, 'behave like a rabbi's son!'

Aaron burst out laughing.

'Adina of course,' sniggered Shlomo.

'Hey,' exclaimed Aaron, 'what's this I hear about Adina getting married?'

'It's true!' Yakov sprang at the sofa again, bouncing up and down till the springs squeaked. 'The groom's called Mordechai Weinberg, and he lives in Warsaw, and his family is coming to inspect her tomorrow!'

'Tomorrow?'

'Yes, and Nomi's all worried because she thinks Adina will have to live in Warsaw. That wouldn't really happen, would it?'

'Well...' Aaron's face grew sombre. 'It depends what Papa agrees with Mordechai's father. At the betrothal ceremony.'

'Oh,' said Yakov. But he couldn't be solemn for long.

'Come on, Shlomo, your turn to pretend,' he said.

Shlomo thought for a minute, then, standing up, seemed to pull something out of his pocket and put it in his mouth. He waited, with his lips pursed. Yakov and Aaron looked at each other.

'Are you supposed to be eating?' asked Aaron.

Shlomo shook his head crossly. He took the imaginary thing from his mouth and blew out air.

'You're smoking!' cried Yakov. 'You're Reb Hirsh.'

'At last!' said Shlomo.

The girls were coming in and out of the room now, sweeping crumbs off the tablecloth, bringing in the clean dishes and cutlery, getting ready for the next meal. They kept looking over at the boys, and every now and then Yochevet exploded in one of her giggles.

Behind them, the doors to the balcony stood ajar, and sunshine poured in, along with gusts of laughter and chatter from other apartments.

Then Mama returned to the dining room, and everyone knew that at any moment Papa would come back too. The girls rushed to get the last few dishes onto the table, Esther went to fetch the little ones from their nap, Mama plumped up the cushions on the sofa, and Shlomo and Yakov hurried to get Papa's chair ready. They each took an arm of the tall, straight-backed chair that stood at

the head of the table and dragged it round to face
the sofa.

'Thank you, boys,' said Papa, marching in and
taking his seat between them.

'Adina, Yochevet,' called Mama. She patted the
cushions either side of her. 'Come sit here where you
can listen comfortably.'

All the girls scrambled to find places kneeling or
leaning around their mother. Aaron plonked himself
in the armchair, and Yakov was about to squeeze in
beside him when Papa spoke again.

'Yakov,' he pronounced, 'we will begin with you.'

Yakov's mouth turned down in a grimace. This
was the part of Shabbes he least enjoyed.

'Tell us what you have learnt this week, Yakov,'
said Papa. 'What was the Torah portion we read in
the shtibel this morning?'

Yakov scuffed the carpet with the toe of his shoe.
It was days since he had done the translation with
his tutor, changing the Hebrew into Yiddish.

'Umm...' he murmured.

'I know!' said Shlomo. 'If—'

'Shlomo,' said Papa. 'It is your brother's turn.'

Yakov glanced helplessly around the room. Nomi
was gazing at him with wide, sympathetic eyes, but
Aaron raised an eyebrow and pretended to stab the
air. Remembrance flooded through him.

'Swords!' he exclaimed. 'If you obey the laws, you can pursue your enemies with swords, and five people will be able to kill one hundred enemies!'

Mama looked pleased, and Papa's lips twitched. 'We-ell,' he murmured, 'it did mention swords and fighting, but the main—'

'I know!' Shlomo interrupted, and broke into a fast, excited gabble. '"If you follow My statutes and observe My commandments and perform them, I will give you rains in their time, the land will yield its produce and the tree of the field will give forth its fruit."'

'Thank you, Shlomo,' said Papa. 'It wasn't your turn, but that is correct. Now...' He leaned back, and clasped his hands over his stomach. 'Let me tell you a parable. There was once a king, who employed four artists...'

With a grin of relief, Yakov cast himself in the chair beside Aaron. His big brother promptly tried to push him off again, but Yakov just let out a chuckle and wriggled in tighter.

'The first artist,' Papa was saying, 'painted a wall of flowers. Day and night he worked...'

Shlomo, leaning on the arm of Papa's chair, listened intently, while Yakov, muffling his giggles, jostled with his big brother Aaron. Yakov felt lightheaded and free. Question time was over for another Shabbes and now he could relax and have fun for the rest of the afternoon.

## Chapter 12

# Nightfall

'I can't see any stars,' Devorah complained.

'Keep watching,' said Nomi.

The two girls were on the balcony overlooking the courtyard, their heads tilted back to peer at the darkening sky. Around them, the wings of the apartment block rose ghostly silver in the twilight, and on every floor other children too leaned against balustrades or peeked through their windows. They were all watching the sky, for when three stars appeared, it would mean that Shabbes was coming to an end.

Suddenly, Devorah let out a yelp. 'There!'

Nomi frowned, and then she too made out the tiny pinpricks of stars.

'Mama!' Devorah turned to rush inside, then stopped. 'Adina?' she queried in surprise.

Their oldest sister was huddled against the wall, her arms clutched across her chest.

'What's wrong?' cried Nomi.

Adina shook her head. 'It's nothing. It's just... It's nearly Sunday,' she said.

Nomi stared at her, and then gasped. Of course! With all the excitement of Shabbes, she had forgotten the visitors.

'What's wrong with Sunday?' demanded Devorah.

'You remember, Mrs Weinberg is coming,' wailed Adina. 'To inspect me!'

'Oh,' said Devorah.

Nomi sympathetically reached out to clasp her big sister's hand, but Devorah tugged them impatiently into the dining room.

'Mama, Esther, Miriam,' she carolled, 'the stars are out.'

Ahead of them, the room melted away into blackness. The candles Mama had lit the night before had long since sputtered and died. Mrs Rabinovitch and the others were vague shapes in the shadows, and when Bluma lifted her head from Mama's shoulder, her eyes were dark pools in a moon-coloured face.

'All right, you can get the Havdalah things ready,' said Mama.

The girls dived for the credenza, giggling as they felt for objects in the dark.

'I've got the candle!' crowed Nomi, brandishing the special candle made of three long tapers twisted together.

'Not much use without these,' taunted Miriam, rattling the matchbox.

'I've got the spice box,' beamed Esther.

'I've got the wine,' said Adina.

'I can't reach,' complained Devorah.

'Here.' Esther placed the silver wine cup in her outstretched hand. 'Can you manage the tray as well?' she asked.

Papa, Yakov and Shlomo arrived from the Prayer House, and the whole family crowded round the head of the table.

'*Baruch ata Adonai, hamavdil bein kodesh l'chol,*' they chanted together. 'Blessed be the One who separates the Sabbath from the working week.'

Nomi held out the candle, her heart quickening with excitement.

Adina grabbed Yakov so he couldn't lean too close.

Miriam struck a match, and the three entwined wicks burst into a leaping flame – the first light of the new week.

Papa started to pour out the wine – and kept on pouring till it spilled over the top of the cup and onto the tray. Then he lifted the cup, and began the prayers.

Esther handed him the spice box. He blessed it, sniffed the cloves, and offered it to the rest of the family to smell.

When he turned to the candle, Nomi held it high and everyone leaned towards it, checking the light was bright enough to show their fingernails. Even little Bluma stretched out her hands.

'*Baruch ata...*' sang Papa.

He lifted the wine cup to his lips. Nomi drew in her breath. Slowly, cautiously, she tilted the candle towards the tray. Papa took a long drink of wine, then turned over the cup, tipping the dregs on the flame. With a loud hiss and splutter, the fire went out. The aroma of melting wax and hot wine joined the scent of cloves.

Sighing with satisfaction, Nomi laid down the candle.

Instantly, everyone jostled to dip their little fingers in the spilled wine and smear it on their eyelids.

'Have a good week,' they called.

'A lucky week,' said Nomi, glancing at Adina.

'A healthy week.'

'A happy week.'

'Girls, back to work!' cried Mama. Thrusting Bluma into Esther's arms, she picked up the spice box and wine bottle and glanced at Devorah, who was stifling a huge yawn. 'Devorah,' she snapped, 'help clear the table. Nomi, put out the fresh tablecloth and candles. Miriam, light the lamps. *Nu*, Adina, why are you just standing there? Go start the soup.'

The Sabbath had to be farewelled in style. Only when the Melave Malke meal was prepared and eaten would Shabbes be truly over. And only then could they all go to bed.

## Chapter 13

# It's today!

NOMI'S EYES FLEW OPEN AND she sat up in bed.

'It's today!' she shrieked. She glanced at the silent form curled up in the other bed. 'Esther, wake up,' she cried. 'It's today!'

'*Modah anee lefanecha*...' Esther muttered, opening her eyes.

Hastily, Nomi joined in the morning prayer, then the two sisters leapt out of bed and jostled for the jug at the washstand.

The moment they finished the blessing, Nomi burst out again.

'Adina will be scared stiff!' she exclaimed.

She gave a shiver of excitement as she dragged on her clothes.

'I wish she didn't have to wear an old dress,' sighed Esther.

'She's got that new ribbon to sew on.'

'Yes, but...people in Warsaw are really smart and fashionable.'

'Oh.' Nomi frowned as she tied the bows on her plaits.

'Your parting's crooked,' warned Esther, picking up the comb.

'No it isn't.'

'Yes it is! Mrs Weinberg will think you're nothing but a tailor's daughter.'

Nomi squirmed out of her sister's grasp and raced for the door. 'Mrs Weinberg won't see me,' she called back. 'Didn't you hear? Mama says we all have to stay out of the salon when the visitors come.'

She heard Esther's wail of disappointment as she bounded down the corridor.

In the kitchen, Adina was measuring sugar and pouring it into a bowl.

'Is that the honey cake?' Nomi rushed across to peer over the edge.

'Get your hair out of it!' screeched her big sister.

'My hair's nowhere near it. Can I help?'

'No, of course not,' snapped Adina. 'It has to be

*my* cake. They're coming to inspect *me*, remember?'

Nomi glanced at Miriam, filling a saucepan with potatoes. They both rolled their eyes.

Mama bustled in, her head wrapped in a checked scarf and her sleeves rolled to the elbows.

'Miriam, what are you doing? I told you to polish the silver.'

'I'm getting breakfast, Mama. Papa will be home in a minute.'

Mrs Rabinovitch glanced at the clock on the mantelpiece.

'Is that the time?' she gasped. 'Nomi, you do the polishing then.' She shoved a rag into Nomi's hand, then snatched it back again. 'No, you better go fetch the bagels. Oy, there is so much to do!'

When Papa returned from the shtibel, he took no notice of the frenzy in his household. He plodded through his breakfast and leaned back to tell a long story from the Torah, ignoring Mama's impatient glances.

At last he began the grace after meals, and the instant his words died away, Mama leapt to her feet.

'Miriam, Yakov, help clear,' she ordered, and barged towards the kitchen with an armload of dishes. 'Nomi, you do the silver,' she shouted back over her shoulder.

Nomi fetched the tea things out of the sideboard

and arranged the tin of polish and the rags on a corner of the dining table.

A crash and a squawk came from the kitchen.

'Ach, Yakov, you klutz!' cried Mama. 'Get out of my way. And don't touch those chocolates. Adina, take this cake tray to Nomi.'

Adina hurried into the dining room, and dumped a silver tray on the table.

Then she spun round. 'Mama,' she cried, 'is Lidia going to bring in my honey cake?'

'Of course not,' Mama called back. 'It's her day off.'

'Who's going to bring it in then?'

Her mother appeared in the doorway. 'No one. The cake will just sit on the table.'

'But...' Adina's face crumpled. 'It will look grander if someone carries it in.'

There was a pause. Mama pursed her lips, then they both looked at Nomi.

'Nomi, is your Shabbes dress clean?' asked Mama.

Nomi's heart seemed to flip in her chest. 'Yes, Mama.'

'There you are then,' said Mama. 'Nomi can bring it. Now go sew the ribbon on your dress, Adina.'

Nomi stared after them, trembling in excitement. She was going to see the Weinbergs after all!

## Chapter 14

# Inspection of the Bride

'YOU ARE SO LUCKY,' SAID Esther. It was afternoon, and she was sitting on Nomi's bed watching her sister change into her Shabbes dress, while Bluma and Devorah played on the floor around them. 'Promise me you'll memorise every single thing they're wearing.'

'I'll try,' said Nomi. 'A-augh, don't let Bluma chew on that!' She grabbed a pink ribbon out of Bluma's mouth, but it was too late. The wide strip of silk taffeta, carefully ironed by Adina, was now crumpled and soggy.

'I'm sorry,' wailed Esther. 'Here, have mine.'

She tugged the ribbon off her own plait and jumped up to tie it in Nomi's hair.

At that moment, there came a rapping at the front door. They both froze, staring at each other.

'They're here!'

There was a faint sound of voices and footsteps in the front hall.

'Quick, get the cake!' cried Esther, pushing her sister towards the door.

'No ... it's all right; they don't need it straight away,' stammered Nomi.

But she hurried anyway, her heart thumping. If I'm nervous, what must Adina be feeling? she thought.

In the kitchen, Miriam was sorting out the heaps of dirty plates and cutlery dumped on the table after lunch.

'I'm left to do this by myself,' she grumbled when Nomi burst through the door.

In the midst of the jumble, the honey cake glistened like a huge dark jewel on its silver tray.

As Nomi reached to pick it up, Miriam let out a yelp, and almost dropped a stack of plates. 'Yakov,' she squawked, 'don't pull my apron!'

There was a scuffling sound under the table, and Yakov peeked out. At the sight of Nomi, his face split in a wide grin, displaying bright orange teeth.

Nomi gaped, and Yakov exploded with laughter, shooting an orange peel out of his mouth.

'Where did you get that orange?' Nomi demanded.

'Mama gave it to me.'

'It was supposed to keep him out of mischief,' snorted Miriam.

Shaking her head, Nomi lifted up the tray.

'Adina makes the best honey cake!' she said, breathing in the delicious caramel scent. 'Yakov, come and open the doors for me.'

'Okay.'

Yakov bobbed to his feet and danced ahead of her, throwing open the door to the other apartment. Itsek began to rise from his chair, but Yakov beat him to the door of the salon.

'Wait!' squeaked Nomi, as her little brother reached out to turn the handle. 'Make sure they don't see you!'

Grinning, he shuffled behind the door and edged it open so she could slip inside.

The salon was filled with sunlight for once. It poured through the open curtains, sending a shower of rainbows sprinkling from the crystal chandelier. They bounced off every shining surface, from the shining black ebony of the tabletop, to the gilt-framed mirror hanging on the wall, to the glass-fronted doors of the china cabinets.

Adina was seated on the yellow satin sofa by the French windows. Her hair was lightly drawn back from her face by a huge bow of green ribbon. She had one of Miriam's long necklaces strung around her neck, and a large rosette of the same ribbon stitched to the shoulder of her pale blue dress. She looked as beautiful as a queen.

But the visitors were not attractive at all. They had pointy noses and dark, old-fashioned dresses (Esther will be disappointed, thought Nomi) and they were perched on the black ebony chairs like a ring of attacking crows. They all looked alike. Which one was the groom's mother?

'Too slow!' the skinniest crow squawked, leaning forward and jabbing the prospective bride with a claw-like finger. Was that one Mrs Weinberg?

Two patches of crimson flared on Adina's cheeks. She was trying to untangle a piece of string, a test to show how patient and diligent she could be.

Nomi bit her lip.

'Nomi!' Mama exclaimed, catching sight of her in the doorway. '*Nu*, don't just stand there. Put the cake on the table.'

Conscious of all the eyes watching her, Nomi crossed the soft green rug and carefully set down her precious burden.

'Look at that, Mrs Weinberg,' gushed Mama. 'Have

you ever seen a more perfect honey cake? Adina baked it herself.'

The four visitors bent forward, peering with beady black eyes and disapproving expressions. The old one (with a wig like a messy bird's nest) had to be Mordechai's grandmother, and the other two must be his aunts. None of them wore jewellery, and their dresses were bare of lace or beading. They looked dowdy next to the Rabbi's wife in her sleek Shabbes wig and diamond brooch.

It was the scrawniest one who spoke again. 'Honey cake?' she quavered. She pursed her lips and frowned. 'It's too dark. And where is the icing?'

Nomi bristled, but Mama was ever the gracious hostess. 'You must taste it, Mrs Weinberg,' she said. 'Adina, cut it for us, please.'

Adina threw down the knotted string and sprang to her feet. Nomi could see her fighting back tears as she came towards the table.

'Your cake is perfect!' Nomi hissed.

'She doesn't think so,' mumbled Adina.

'She's just stupid.'

Adina managed a watery smile, but when she handed Mrs Weinberg the first slice, she lifted her chin up proudly.

'Enjoy,' she said.

Mama caught Nomi's eye and inclined her head towards the door.

Reluctantly, Nomi took a step backwards. The groom's mother was just taking a bite...

To Nomi's utter disbelief, Mrs Weinberg clanked the plate down and pushed it away. 'Too dry,' she pronounced. 'Mine is better!'

Seething, Nomi spun on her heel, and stomped out of the room.

Yakov was waiting behind the door.

'I hope they didn't see you,' Nomi whispered, pushing it shut.

'I hope they did. I poked my tongue out at them.'

'You *what*?!'

Yakov pursed his lips, mimicking Mrs Weinberg. 'Too slow!' he screeched, stabbing Nomi with his finger at each word. 'Too dark! Too dry!'

'Sssh,' gasped Nomi, 'they'll hear you!'

She glanced, embarrassed, at Itsek, then grabbing her little brother by the arm, she tugged him into the other hallway, where a mob of impatient, excited siblings was waiting to pounce.

'Did you see them?' hissed Shlomo.

'What were they like?' demanded Miriam.

'Did you bring me lollies?' shrilled Devorah.

'What were they wearing?' (That was Esther.)

Nomi opened her mouth.

'Mrs Weinberg is *awful*,' burst in Yakov.

'And I don't think she likes Adina,' added Nomi.

There was a dumbfounded silence.

Then, 'A rabbi's daughter rejected by a *saucepan maker*?' mourned Shlomo.

'Good, then she won't have to marry that Mordechai person,' said Miriam.

'Miriam, how can you say that? Mama will die of shame,' groaned Esther.

'And what about Adina?' demanded Nomi. She clenched her fists. 'That Weinberg woman is a cow!'

'No she's not. She's a pig!' snorted Yakov. 'Oink oink!'

'She's a bedbug,' growled Devorah in a deep, indignant voice.

They stared at each other with worried faces. What on earth would they say to Adina when she came back again?

At last, from behind the communicating door, came a buzz of voices.

'It's them!'

The children strained to hear. There came a cackling laugh – 'Mrs Weinberg!' mouthed Nomi – and then the front door clicked shut. The next instant, Mama, Papa and Adina were in the hallway with the rest of the family.

Mama was holding out her arms for hugs, laughing and crying at the same time. 'My first daughter is going to be married!' she burbled.

Adina looked dazed, while Papa beamed and stroked his beard.

'But, Mama—' protested Miriam. 'Nomi said that Mrs Weinberg doesn't like Adina.'

Mrs Rabinovitch swelled up with indignation. 'Not like a daughter of *mine*?' she demanded.

Nomi blushed. 'I didn't…She didn't…' she stammered.

'Ach, every groom's mother has to criticise,' said Mama, blowing her nose on her handkerchief. 'It is expected. I did the same to Yochevet.'

They all stared at her.

'You mean she *does* like Adina?' asked Esther.

'Of course she does. The wedding is arranged for September.'

'God willing,' said the Rabbi.

## Chapter 15

# The Dowry

THE NEXT MORNING, STRAIGHT AFTER breakfast, the sisters crammed excitedly into Miriam and
Adina's bedroom.

'Adina, did you find out more about Mordechai?'

'What date is the wedding?'

'What did Mrs Weinberg *say*?'

'Everyone, stop talking at once!' cried Adina. 'Yes,
I found out more about Mordechai. He is seventeen,
and...'

'Will you have to live in Warsaw?' Nomi interrupted.

'I don't know. They'll work it out at the betrothal.'

'But...'

'What's a trothal?' asked Devorah.

'It's when the groom comes here and meets Papa and they plan my dowry and where we will live.'

'*That's* your dowry,' said the four-year-old, pointing at one of the two painted chests that stood between the beds.

'Yes, you're right, only…Papa will have to pay some money as well.'

'Why?'

'Because that's what happens.'

'Why?'

Adina blew out her cheeks.

'Don't be annoying, Devorah,' said Esther. 'Adina, show us your dowry.'

Everyone crowded around as the bride-to-be bent to unlock the chest.

'You're not going to believe what's inside,' said Miriam. 'Adina spends *hours* sewing.'

With a flourish, Adina pushed back the lid, and Esther and Nomi gasped.

'I told you,' said Miriam. 'Look.' She pulled out a tablecloth of pure white linen edged all the way around with tiny, perfect stitches.

'Adina, that must have taken you forever,' exclaimed Esther.

'I can't see,' complained Devorah, trying to peer between her sisters.

'Let's put everything on the bed,' suggested Adina; and then, 'Careful!' she protested, as eager hands dived in to pull things out.

'These are beautiful,' breathed Nomi. Gently, she spread out two pillowcases decorated with lace fringes.

'Ooh, look what I found!' Almost toppling into the box, Devorah scooped out a bag of coins and danced with it across the room. 'I'm the richest person,' she sang out.

'Don't you lose that,' called Adina, laughing. 'And Bluma, that's not for chewing on.' The baby had pulled herself up and was gnawing the wooden edge of the chest. Adina plucked her off and dumped her on all fours. 'Go crawl,' she said.

One by one, the contents were exclaimed over, and strewn on the bed. There were fat, puffy pillows, a feather eiderdown, and a dozen linen napkins embroidered with Adina's initials. Esther drew out lengths of dress fabrics in blue and violet and green and held them against herself in the mirror.

Then she lifted up a sheet, and frowned.

'This one's not hemmed,' she said.

The bright smile faded from Adina's face. 'Uh… I haven't finished the sheets yet,' she muttered.

'What, *none* of them?!'

Adina turned pink.

'But your wedding is in three months!'

'I know.' Suddenly a cry of anguish broke from Adina. 'I can't possibly do them all in time,' she wailed. 'And I have to sew presents for the bridegroom too, like the bag to keep his prayer shawl in.'

They all stared at her.

'I'll help you,' said Esther. 'We all will.'

'Speak for yourself,' growled Miriam.

Nomi's heart sank. She could never sew as well as Adina.

And, 'I don't know how to sew,' whimpered Devorah.

'You can look after Bluma,' said Esther. 'Come on, everyone. Let's start right now.'

The sisters arranged themselves in twos, Adina and Miriam on one bed, and Esther and Nomi on the other, each with a sheet that needed hemming draped across her knee. Bluma and Devorah disappeared under Miriam's bed with muffled thumps and squeaks.

'What am I doing this for?' grumbled Miriam, yanking the needle through her cloth with a rough, angry jerk.

'So Adina can get married,' said Esther.

'Huh,' huffed Miriam, 'to some baboon she's never met.' She stabbed the needle in again.

'I am sure Mama and Papa will not choose a baboon,' said Esther firmly.

Nomi cast an anxious glance at Adina. What was her big sister thinking?

'A...dina,' she faltered, 'do you *want* to get married?'

Adina's mouth pressed into a thin, tight line and for a moment she didn't answer.

Then, 'I think so,' she blurted out.

'You think so?' exploded Esther. 'Of course you want to. You get to wear a beautiful bride dress and have your own home and everything.' She gave Nomi a nudge. 'Stop asking silly questions,' she hissed. 'Come on, you're supposed to be sewing.'

Nomi thought miserably of the grubby, badly sewn efforts in her own dowry chest. Sighing, she picked up her needle and plunged it into the perfect white linen.

'Ouch!' she squeaked.

Adina's head shot up. 'Don't get blood on there!' she cried.

Hastily, Nomi put her hand over the red dot.

At that moment, the bride-to-be let out a yelp. Bluma had crawled into view and was tugging on her sewing.

'Bluma, let go,' she scolded. 'Devorah, where are you? What are you doing?'

The four-year-old wriggled from under the bed and stamped to her feet, dusty and dishevelled.

'I don't *want* to look after Bluma any more,' she complained.

Adina heaved a sigh. 'Esther, you'd better take them outside,' she said.

'But...' Esther gazed, crestfallen, at the sewing in her hands.

'I'll take them!' cried Nomi and Miriam, leaping up together.

With an eager lunge, Nomi scooped Bluma from the ground. 'Come on Bluma, come on Devorah,' she whooped. 'Let's get out of here.' Throwing Miriam a grin of triumph, she escaped from the room.

## Chapter 16

# The Betrothal

THE NEXT FEW WEEKS SPED BY, and almost before they knew it, the day of the betrothal had arrived. Mama whirled about the salon, tweaking, rearranging and barking instructions, while her daughters and daughter-in-law piled dishes on the table and frantically polished finger-marks off the shiny ebony furniture.

The boys tried to keep out of the way, but, 'Aaron, Shlomo, Yakov, make yourselves useful,' cried Mama. 'You, Shlomo, put out the brandy and glasses. Aaron, bring in more chairs. Yakov...' She swept a full jug off the sideboard and thrust it into his hands. 'Water the flowers.'

Yakov stared at the vase of roses on the tall stand beside him. The top of it was higher than he was. With difficulty, he hoisted the heavy crystal jug to the rim, and tilted. Water spouted everywhere.

'Yakov!' howled Adina. 'Not those flowers. On the balcony.' She slapped at the spilled water with her polishing cloth.

'Oh.'

The balcony off the salon was Mama's pride and joy. Unlike the balcony from the dining room, this one jutted onto the street, so Mama filled it with plants to impress the passers-by: flourishing oleander bushes in wooden tubs, waterfalls of fuchsias from hanging baskets, and a forest of pansies in a planter box attached to the rail.

But today, with the sun beating down, the pansies were drooping like a row of noodles hung up to dry. Humming, Yakov began to water them.

In the street below, a large droshky came to a halt at the kerb. Yakov glanced down with interest as people began to descend: men in long Shabbes jackets of black silk, and women with jewels around their necks. One of the women looked like ...

Letting out a whoop, Yakov dropped the water jug among the pansies, and raced back through the long French windows.

'They're here!' he shouted. 'They're coming in the gate!'

'What?! Already?!' Mama threw up her arms. 'Quick, girls, into the waiting room,' she gasped.

Adina cast a desperate glance over her shoulder as she was shooed towards the door. 'Yakov, come and tell me what he's like!' she cried.

'And find out if he has to stay in Warsaw,' called Nomi.

'Go, go,' urged Mama.

As soon as they disappeared, Yakov's hand flicked out to grab a slice of orange.

'Yakov, it is polite to wait for the guests,' rumbled his father's voice.

Guiltily, Yakov dropped his hand.

At that moment there came a rap at the door, the scuff of Itsek's footsteps, and a surge of voices.

The next instant, a group of strange men were ushered into the salon, and beyond them Yakov could see the women guests going into the waiting room across the hallway.

'Reb Weinberg, Mordechai,' cried the Rabbi, clasping hands in welcome.

Yakov gaped at the young man who was about to become his brother-in-law. He had a long, thick beard, even though he was only Aaron's age, but the most startling thing about him was its colour: it was a bright, carroty red.

He caught his older brother's eye, and Aaron twitched his eyebrows.

'Now, Reb Weinberg, we must talk—' said Papa, and placing a hand under the other father's elbow, he guided him towards a corner of the room.

Mordechai watched them go with a nervous expression, then turned to face the three Rabinovitch brothers ranged in front of him.

'How much Torah do you know?' demanded Shlomo. 'I can recite the portion from Saturday by heart. Listen.'

But before he could begin, Aaron interrupted him.

'I am sure Mordechai knows that too,' he said.

'Of course,' said Mordechai, and rattled off a stream of Hebrew.

Shlomo crossed his arms. 'So, what does it say in the Talmud about it?'

Mordechai Weinberg drew in his breath. 'It says...'

Yakov's attention wandered. He didn't know any Talmud yet – all those explanations and laws – but he did know the Torah story. His tutor had translated it from Hebrew to Yiddish for him. He liked the bit about the earth opening up, and everyone getting swallowed up in a pit of fire...

Meanwhile, the guests were milling around, feasting, chatting, and filling the room with cigar smoke.

Yakov watched anxiously as the piles on the plates grew smaller. At last, unable to resist, he darted to the table, wolfed down a slice of poppy-seed cake, and picked up another one for Mordechai.

Worming his way back to the others, he waved the slice under the bridegroom's nose. 'Here. Adina baked it,' he declared, though he had no idea if this was true.

The redhead abruptly stopped talking and cupped his hands to catch the broken bits of cake Yakov was showering into them.

'It's...delicious,' he mumbled, blushing as he tried to brush the crumbs off his beard and long black coat.

Shlomo opened his mouth to ask another question and Yakov cut in quickly. 'Mordechai, are you and Adina going to live in Warsaw or here?' he demanded.

The young man looked startled. 'I...don't know.' He shot a glance at the two fathers conferring in a corner. 'My father expects me to join his business. Only...' He lowered his voice. 'I just want to study Torah. I'd rather spend my days in a Prayer House.'

'Here in Lublin?' asked Yakov eagerly.

The groom blushed darker. 'That's what I hope. Your father is a rabbi. I would like to study under his guidance, if I could.'

'Ooh, I have to tell Nomi. And Adina,' cried Yakov.

At that moment, Itsek burst into their midst, looking distraught.

'Where's the Rabbi?' he rasped.

'There.'

The brothers stared after him as he plunged through the crowd and caught hold of their father's arm. A rare frown creased the Rabbi's face and he glanced towards the door. The boys turned to look too, and their jaws dropped.

A policeman was standing in the entranceway.

'Yakov, what have you done?' moaned Shlomo.

'Why me?' protested Yakov.

When the sergeant stomped through the door, it seemed as if a bolt from a Bible story was striking the room. Everyone fell back, silent and staring.

The man barged forward, helmet pressed low on his forehead, and chinstrap tight around his jutting jowls.

He reached Papa, and jerked his thumb at the balcony.

'Yid!' he spat. Then he spewed out a stream of Polish.

Yakov caught the word '*woda*' and his heart sank.

'He says that water from our balcony is dripping on people in the street,' hissed Aaron.

Mordechai's eyes grew round as saucers and Shlomo looked accusingly at Yakov. 'You put too much water on the plants,' he growled.

'One złoty,' finished the policeman with a snarl, thrusting out a hand.

Slowly, with a stony face, Papa slid his fingers into his pocket, drew out a coin and dropped it on the outstretched palm.

The policeman gave a snort, and stormed out of the room.

In the stunned, uncomfortable silence, the sound of women's laughter drifted from the waiting room.

Yakov's stomach tightened. The women didn't even know yet that a policeman had ruined the betrothal.

All the guests are going to leave now, he thought miserably.

The Rabbi cleared his throat. 'Well, Reb Weinberg—' he began.

Someone else let out an embarrassed laugh, and a few voices began to murmur. In a moment, the room was filled with noise and chatter again. Yakov looked around, astonished. Everyone was going on as if nothing had happened.

'Well.' Aaron clapped his hands together. 'There's plenty of food left. Shall we eat?'

'Yes!'

Yakov reached the table in one bound, but as he eagerly helped himself to gingerbread, he remembered his sisters waiting for news.

I'd better go, he thought, and cramming the whole piece in his mouth, he raced towards the door.

Gusts of perfume and laughter met him at the threshold to the waiting room. He stretched on his toes, trying to see into the crowd of silk-clad women, then suddenly Nomi was in front of him, her words tumbling together. 'Did you ... What did you ... What did you find out? What's Mordechai like? Did you ask him about coming to Lublin?'

Yakov licked the last crumbs off his fingers. 'He's got a bright red beard, and he wants to come to Lublin ...'

'Ooh,' cried Nomi, bouncing up and down. 'Come and tell Adina.'

They squeezed through the crowd, almost tripping on Adina's dowry box, open in the middle of the floor. Yakov had a glimpse of Devorah with a chocolate-smeared mouth being pulled away from it by a hot and bothered Esther, and Mama, regal and bejewelled, showing off a pillowcase to Mrs Weinberg.

'Excuse me, excuse me,' cried Nomi.

They reached Adina, and Nomi reached out to prod her sister's arm. 'Adina, look who's here,' she crowed.

Adina turned with a reproving frown, and caught sight of her brother.

'Yakov!' She flung out her hands and pulled him close. 'Tell me Mordechai is nice,' she pleaded.

Yakov nodded eagerly. 'Yes, he...'

'He's got a red beard!' Nomi interrupted. 'And...'

But at that moment there was a commotion on the other side of the room.

'They've decided!' cried excited voices.

Yakov saw Adina's face turn white.

Papa and Reb Weinberg were coming through the crowd, and the Rabbi had a rolled-up parchment in his hand.

'Reb Weinberg, let me introduce... the bride,' said Papa, and waved his arm with a flourish.

'Delighted,' murmured Mordechai's short, portly father with a bow.

The Rabbi looked at the whispering, jostling crowd, and raised the parchment in the air. 'The betrothal conditions are agreed,' he called out. 'The honourable and learned student Mordechai will marry my daughter Adina (long may she live) according to the laws of Moses and Israel. May they be honest with each other, and live in love and harmony.

'It is agreed that Reb Weinberg will provide his son, the bridegroom, with Sabbath and Holy Day clothes and I will pay the expenses for the wedding. And also...' He paused to beam at his daughter. 'I will support the groom in his studies, and provide the young couple with a home, here in Lublin...'

'Papa!' gasped Adina. Colour flooded her cheeks.

'Mazel tov!' shrieked Mrs Rabinovitch.

'Mazel tov!' cried Mrs Weinberg.

The two mothers snatched up a large platter together, and hurled it to the floor with a CRASH of splintering china.

Yakov jumped in shock, and then he remembered that Mama and Yochevet's mother had done the same at Aaron's betrothal. Maybe it frightened away demons or something.

Everyone broke into shouts of congratulation.

Mordechai's father unfurled a heavy gold chain from his pocket.

'A gift for the bride,' he wheezed, and Mrs Weinberg proudly draped it around Adina's neck.

'And I have a gift for Mordechai,' responded Papa, pulling a gold watch and chain out of his own pocket. 'A Swiss Schaffhausen watch!' he announced proudly.

The two men made their way to the door again, but Yakov paused to watch Adina as she smiled happily and swayed from side to side to show off her necklace. Esther was hoisting up the little ones to touch the gold, and Nomi was jigging with excitement...

Suddenly, he found himself clutched in Mama's arms and pressed against her damp cheek. As usual, Mama was laughing and crying at the same time.

Embarrassed, Yakov wriggled free, and fled from the room.

Back in the salon, Papa and Reb Weinberg were the centre of a mob of cheering, excited men, everyone thumping them on the back and shouting, 'Mazel tov! Mazel tov!'

When Yakov appeared, someone swept him into the air and danced him around on his shoulders, and Yakov hung on, almost falling off, laughing and shouting with everyone else. He caught a glimpse of Mordechai, with his face pink and shiny, tossing back an amber-coloured tot of brandy, and Aaron trying to do a Cossack dance with a bottle on his head.

Then everyone threw themselves at the furniture, shoving it aside to make room for dancing. Gleefully, Yakov joined in as they hurled the delicate ebony chairs into higgledy-piggledy piles, and tipped the yellow satin sofa on its end.

Someone broke into song, and the men dashed to form a circle. Slinging their arms about each other's shoulders, they began to dance around the room, and Yakov joined in.

Round they whirled, faster and faster. Their boots thundered on the floor. Furniture toppled. Crockery rattled. Yakov's arms were almost pulled out of their sockets, his toes bruised by pounding feet. But he didn't care. Stamping and singing at the top of his voice, he joined in the celebrations for the betrothal of his sister Adina to Mordechai Weinberg.

## Chapter 17

# The Picnic

'I'M HOT,' COMPLAINED DEVORAH.

'Well, so am I,' snapped Miriam. She let out a groan as Mama, Esther and Adina stopped at yet another fabric stall, then she dropped her basket, and sank down beside it.

After a moment's hesitation, Nomi joined her. Mama would scold them for sitting on the filthy cobblestones of the market, but Nomi didn't care. She was too hot and tired.

It was the middle of August. They should have been in the country for their summer holiday. But because of the wedding, they had all been obliged to stay in town.

'Who will write the invitations and organise the food?' Mama had exclaimed, when Nomi asked about going to the farm. 'Do you think they just arrange themselves?'

When at last they finished their shopping, and trudged up the stairs of number 30, they were surprised to see Papa coming out to greet them, a smile stretched across his face.

'I have arranged a picnic for you,' he announced. 'On Monday.'

'A picnic!' Nomi dropped her packages, grabbed Devorah's hands, and began to dance her around.

Laughing, Esther and Miriam joined in.

'Pic-a-nic, pic-a-nic,' sang Devorah.

But, 'Yehoshua, are you mad?' cried Mrs Rabinovitch. 'We can't go on a picnic.'

Nomi, Devorah, Esther and Miriam skidded to a halt and stared at their mother in dismay.

'Mama,' soothed the Rabbi. 'It is just for one day. This is holiday time, and the children...'

Mrs Rabinovitch threw her hands in the air. 'Holiday?!' she shrieked. 'How can you talk about holidays when we have a wedding in less than four weeks? Anyway, Sura the Dressmaker arrives on Monday, and Adina must be measured for her dress and her trousseau and...'

'So, you and Adina stay here then,' said the Rabbi.

'Lidia will take the younger ones on the picnic.'

All through the next two days, every time Nomi thought of their outing, she broke into a smile.

On Sunday, Old Chaim brought up the big wicker basket from the cupboard under the stairs. The picnic basket!

On Monday, Nomi woke up even before Papa left for the shtibel. She scampered to the kitchen on her bare feet. Lidia was there already, slicing a fresh-baked loaf for sandwiches.

'It's ... too hot ... to cut,' grumbled the maid.

Lidia's hair was tumbling out of its pins, and her white dress with its print of red roses strained across her back as she sawed at the bread.

'I'll help.' Nomi picked up the rough chunks of bread, squeaking as they burnt her fingers, and smeared them with butter. Then she wrapped them in napkins and packed them in the hamper.

Lidia added hard-boiled eggs, a babka loaf glazed with cinnamon and brown sugar, and a thermos of cold tea.

'We don't need tea!' Nomi exclaimed. 'We'll have frothy milk straight from the cow.'

Lidia sniffed. 'I don't drink that stuff,' she said.

As soon as breakfast was over, the children raced for the kitchen, squeaking with excitement. Even Shlomo looked less solemn than usual.

The two boys grasped the handles of the big hamper and hoisted it into the air.

'Let's go!' they cried, jostling their way out the back door.

'Pic-a-nic, pic-a-nic,' chanted Devorah as they turned into Lubartowska Street.

Nomi and Esther caught hold of her hands and the three of them loped along together.

'Pic-a-nic, pic-a-nic, we're going on a pic-a-nic!' they sang.

'Lucky you,' smiled Toiba Grynszpan, brushing past them with a wig box in her arms.

'Have fun,' called Efroyim the Baker, waving from the front of his shop.

At the Krakow Gate though, the children fell silent. This was where the Jewish quarter of Lublin ended. They passed through the archway, and stepped out cautiously on the other side.

Zamojska Street looked just like Lubartowska Street: it had the same tall buildings in shades of pink and yellow, with apartments on the upper floors and shops below, but the Rabinovitches knew this was a different world. Here, there were no signs written in Yiddish, there were no women wearing wigs, and no other boys with long curled sidelocks, or fringes showing beneath their jackets.

As Lidia strode ahead, the children followed in

a tight, uneasy bunch. Passers-by turned to stare at them, and Nomi glared back, her cheeks burning.

'Ignore them,' said Miriam, tossing her hair.

Ahead, along the road, they could see a bridge, a river, and a clump of willow trees.

'Is that the farm?' asked Devorah.

'No, silly, we still have to go on the train.' Esther shot an amused glance at Nomi.

But Nomi didn't smile back. Her eye was caught by a group of boys among the trees. Something about the way they were standing made her stomach tighten.

Sure enough, as the children drew closer, one of the boys pulled back his arm and flung something towards them.

'Hey!' squeaked Esther as a shower of pebbles spattered at her feet.

Then, 'Ouch! Eek! Ow!' they all cried as more and more pebbles came raining down on them.

The whole gang was throwing now, yelling at the tops of their voices.

'Yids, yids, yids!' they taunted.

Nomi grew hot with anger as she tried to avoid the sharp little stones biting into her arms and legs.

'Throw some back,' yelled Yakov, and dropping his end of the basket, he scrabbled up a fistful of pebbles.

Lidia, who had reached the bridge ahead of them, swung around with a face of fury.

'*Przestańcie!*' she screamed at the louts in Polish. 'Stop that! Go away!'

With a few final jeers, the boys swaggered off among the trees, Yakov angrily trying to hit them with his stones.

Lidia came panting back to her charges. 'Stick... with me,' she gasped. 'All of you.' She grabbed Devorah's hand and began to haul her along. 'Faster, or we'll miss the train!' she urged.

In a few minutes, she was pushing them through the doorway of the station.

'Go wait on the platform,' she ordered, and hurried towards the barred window of the ticket office.

There were flocks of noisy families milling everywhere.

'Lots of people going on picnics!' Devorah exclaimed.

'*They're* probably going away for holidays,' said Nomi, but her words were swept away as a whistle shrilled, and the ground began to tremble.

'The train's coming!' whooped Yakov.

He leapt forward and Nomi had to grab the back of his jacket to stop him vanishing into the crowd.

'Wait for Lidia,' she shouted in his ear.

Down the track came the train, thundering and roaring, larger and larger, noisier and noisier.

Shlomo clapped his hands over his ears, and Devorah buried her face in Esther's dress.

With another shriek and a hiss of steam, the huge engine juddered to a halt. Doors flew open and the crowd surged forward, excited and shouting. For a moment, they tangled with arriving passengers in a mess of arms and legs and bundles, then the chaos cleared, and the Rabinovitch children found themselves alone on the platform.

'Stand back! Stand back!'

A man wearing a blue jacket with shiny brass buttons strode along the carriages, slamming the doors again. The train began to puff and steam.

'They're leaving,' wailed Yakov. 'Where's Lidia?'

At that moment the maid shot up beside him, waving the tickets.

'Come on!'

Grabbing each other's hands, they tumbled on board. The door crashed behind them, and the train began to move.

'Woah!' laughed Yakov, toppling onto the picnic hamper.

The rest of them clung together, swaying and giggling, and looked round hopefully for somewhere to sit.

'*Siedzieć,*' offered a woman in Polish, hoisting her toddler onto her lap.

'Thank you... *Dziękuję!*' gasped Nomi. She and Esther collapsed on the empty seat, gathering Devorah on top of them.

'Listen,' said Nomi excitedly. 'Can you hear the wheels? They're saying *pic-a-nic, pic-a-nic, pic-a-nic.*'

She arched forward, trying to see out the window. Strange buildings flashed past, and trees, and fields. And then a cow!

'Poor Adina's missing out,' she said.

'She doesn't mind. She's got the dressmaker today,' said Esther.

The ticket inspector appeared in the doorway.

'Tickets please!' he demanded.

The engine emitted a long, drawn-out whistle, and as they rounded a curve, a trail of smoke drifted into the carriage. With a loud *bang*, a man snapped the window shut.

'Devorah, you've got soot on your chin,' laughed Esther, and licked her finger to scrub it clean.

At Garbatka station, the Rabinovitches fought their way through the crowd of people getting off, and reached the line of wagons waiting outside the pink-painted building.

'There's Mendel,' shouted Yakov, as one of the wagon drivers raised both arms to wave at them.

Mendel the Farmer was almost as wide as he was tall. He had a long grey beard twisted in two trailing points that flapped when he moved like the tassels swinging from his tsitsis.

'Welcome,' he boomed, jumping from his wagon as the children ran up to him. 'Goodness, haven't you all grown?' He gazed around at them admiringly. 'This couldn't be little Devorah?' He pinched her cheek. 'But, wait, isn't someone missing? There should be one more of you.'

'Yes, Adina.'

'But she couldn't come.'

'She had to stay home for the dressmaker.'

'She's getting married.'

'God willing.' (That was Shlomo.)

'Getting married? Goodness me. You are growing up.'

'And I'm not the littlest any more,' said Devorah. 'There's a baby now, but she's too young for picnics.'

'Well, well.' Mendel shook his head in amazement.

Miriam was stroking the horse's nose. 'Have you something I can feed Dancer?' she asked.

'Of course,' grinned Mendel, and he produced a carrot from a pocket in his baggy brown vest.

'Let's go,' pleaded Nomi impatiently.

The farmer chuckled, tugged one of her plaits, then picked up the picnic hamper and heaved it into the wagon. 'All right, all aboard,' he called. Devorah raised her arms to be lifted. 'Anyone else need a hand?' he asked.

But the other children were already scrambling up and tumbling over the sides of the wagon, giggling and squeaking as stray wisps of hay tickled their noses.

Lidia arranged herself on the bench seat in front, and when Mendel swung up beside her, their two broad figures almost overflowed the bench.

'*Vyo* Dancer!' urged Mendel, giving the reins a flick.

The horse broke into a trot.

'Not so fast!' shrieked Lidia, clutching the edge of her seat. 'We'll overturn.'

'Faster, faster,' called Yakov.

Mendel grinned, and flicked the reins again.

Kneeling up so they could peer over the sides of the wagon, the children watched the scenery fly past. First came the wooden houses of the village. They had steeply pitched roofs and rambling gardens, so different from the apartment blocks of Lublin. Then came the fields and orchards and patches of dark woods.

'Where's the farm? Where's the farm?' demanded Devorah.

'Here it is,' Mendel announced.

The wagon turned in a gate, and rattled and bumped up an earthen track.

'I can see the cow!'

'I can see the hens. Mendel, can we look for eggs?'

'Yes, of course,' smiled the farmer.

Mendel's wife Golde had spread a rug for them among the plum trees in the orchard.

Yakov dropped from the wagon as soon as it stopped moving. 'I'm starving,' he proclaimed.

'Me too.'

'Pic-a-nic time!'

'But it's only morning,' objected Lidia. Waddling to a hammock strung between two trees, she heaved herself into it and closed her eyes.

Nobody paid any attention to Lidia. After all, she wasn't Mama. The girls and Yakov crowded onto the rug and Mendel set down the hamper.

'Wait,' cried Shlomo as Miriam threw open the lid. 'Don't forget the blessing.'

Golde had set out a jug and basin for washing hands. They all jostled for turns, then Shlomo pompously unwrapped a sandwich and, holding it up for everyone to see, he recited the blessing over bread.

Sunlight sparkled through the trees. Insects hummed, a cow mooed, and the air smelled of warm hay and ripe plums. Behind the farmhouse, a field of cut wheat stretched into the distance, with a few lone ears left standing in a corner for anyone who was needy.

Nomi gazed around her, and thought how different it felt to give thanks for food from the earth when she could see it growing right there in front of her.

'Amen,' she sang out fervently, then she tore the wrapping off a sandwich and sank her teeth into the soft, fresh bread.

'Mmm,' she sighed. 'Picnic food tastes better than other food.'

'Have some plums, too,' said Mendel the Farmer, reaching up to pick a handful from the branch over his head.

'Can I climb the trees and pick more?' asked Yakov.

'Of course.'

'Are the wild strawberries ripe?' asked Esther.

Mendel nodded and smiled.

'We can pick strawberries in the woods, and feed Dancer, and look for eggs, and milk the cow,' murmured Nomi happily. 'This is a perfect picnic!'

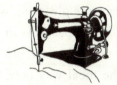

## Chapter 18

# Preparations

THE NEXT MORNING, NOMI WOKE to the clackety-clack of a sewing machine. Sura the Dressmaker was already at work. Fabrics, patterns, scissors and buttons were scattered all over the dining room.

At lunchtime everyone had to squeeze in to eat around the table in the kitchen.

Papa picked up his spoon, looked at his family, and announced, 'Praise God, I have found an apartment for Adina and Mordechai.'

Everyone gasped.

'Where?' demanded Yakov.

The Rabbi took a sip of his soup and a bite of bread before he answered. 'Right here in this building,' he answered. 'On the third floor.'

Nomi felt a rush of relief. Adina would be living just at the top of the stairs! She glanced at her big sister. Adina's eyes were glittering with happy tears.

'I have the key,' said Papa. 'We can see it after lunch.'

The children nudged each other to eat faster, and as soon as the meal was over, they charged up the stairs, then hung impatiently over the banister waiting for Papa and Mama to join them.

'This one,' puffed Papa, arriving at the top.

He unlocked a yellow-painted door and led the way in.

With squeals of excitement, the rest of the family set off around the apartment.

'Hellooo, hellooo!' hollered Yakov, stomping his feet to hear the echoes, and kicking up clouds of dust in the empty rooms.

There were three tiny bedrooms, a kitchen and a dining room.

'Like a doll's house,' said Nomi.

'Yehoshua, it's filthy,' muttered Mama when they all arrived back at the front door.

'Ach, it just needs a good clean and a coat of paint,' said Papa.

Nomi looked at her big sister.

But gradually, one by one, things began to be ready. The bride dress was finished and hung in Miriam and Adina's bedroom. The painters packed up and took themselves off, leaving an odour of calcimine, and gleaming new walls. Men with rolled-up sleeves and bulging muscles tramped up the stairs delivering the furniture.

'Look how sleek and modern everything is!' purred Mama.

At last, on the first Friday of September, just four days before the wedding, the rattle of the sewing machine came to an end.

'Finished!' cried Sura, throwing up her hands.

She rolled her scraps together, and picked up her scattered buttons.

'Have a good Shabbes,' she called, and marched out the door.

The Rabinovitch children exploded with elation.

'Sura's gone, Sura's gone,' whooped Yakov, and he galloped around the dining room.

Adina, coming in with a dustcloth, was grabbed by the elbow and pulled into a dance.

'Adina's getting married! Adina's getting married!' Yakov chanted.

'Hey, let me get the room clean for Shabbes!' cried Adina, but she was laughing at the same time.

Nobody in the household could help feeling happy

and excited. Even Miriam was crowing about having a bedroom all to herself in a few days. When Nomi was sent to help make the beds, she threw a fresh, starched sheet over her head and paraded around the room, crying, 'Lidia, look, I'm a bride!'

'Don't you crumple that,' scolded the maid. But she was smiling too.

Mama kept breaking off her work to dash upstairs for another inspection of the apartment, or to pop into the bedroom for another look at the bride dress.

Then she rushed back to her kitchen, exhorting her daughters to help.

'Adina, it's time to make the challahs; Miriam, your soup is boiling over; Nomi, fetch my Shabbes wig. Oy, we'll never be ready for Shabbes in time!'

There was one awful moment when Adina, stepping into her bath, said, 'This is my last bath at home!' and everyone suddenly realised how much they were going to miss her. Even Adina seemed about to cry. Then she scooped up a handful of water and threw it at her sisters, making them squeal and laugh.

'I won't have to put up with sharing your horrible lukewarm water any more!' she grinned.

Somehow, despite all the chaos, the Shabbes chores got done. The challahs came back from the baker, brown and shiny, the snowy tablecloth was laid with crockery and silver, the candlesticks were polished and put ready on the table, and then it was time for Nomi to help Mama choose her jewellery.

She tapped on her mother's bedroom door.

'Come in,' called Mrs Rabinovitch.

The hipbath stood in the middle of the room, still steaming gently, and Mama sat at the dressing-table in a cloud of perfume.

She turned from the mirror, smiling and holding out the linen bag.

'You first,' she said.

One by one Nomi and Mama drew the pearls, rubies, diamonds, silver and gold out of the sawdust and laid them on the dressing-table.

Finally Mama gave the bag a pat and set it aside.

'That's everything,' she sighed. 'Now, what should I wear tonight?'

Nomi stared at the jewellery, then up at her mother's face.

'W-where's my favourite,' she stammered, 'the bird brooch with the diamond wings?'

Mrs Rabinovitch picked up the ruby earrings and held them to her ears.

'What about these?' she said, turning back to the mirror.

'Mama?' Nomi asked again, puzzled.

Her mother slapped the earrings down and snatched up the pearl necklace.

'The brooch is gone, Nomi. I sold it.'

Nomi stared at her mother in disbelief.

'Sold it?'

'Of course. How do you think we paid for Adina's wedding, and the dowry, and the apartment, and everything else? Now, help me do this up.' She swung round, holding up the ends of the necklace.

With a lump in her throat, Nomi lifted her fingers to obey.

Faintly, from the street below, came the cry of Peretz the Shammes, knocking on doors and calling, 'Time to light the candles! Time to light the candles!'

'It's late!' cried Mama. 'Is it fastened?'

'Yes, Mama.'

Mrs Rabinovitch pushed back her chair and headed for the door, while Nomi lingered to pack the other jewels in the sawdust.

'Don't be long, Nomi,' called Mama sharply.

'No, Mama.'

But as Nomi picked up each earring and brooch, she stroked it lovingly before she slipped it in the bag. And when she hurried after her mother, there were tears rolling down her cheeks.

'Don't be a goose,' she told herself crossly. 'Adina being happy is more important than a lump of yellow metal and some glittery old stones.'

She thought of Adina's beaming face as she stood

in her shiny little doll's house of a home looking around. 'That Mordechai Weinberg had better be nice to her,' she growled.

In the dining room, everyone was waiting for her.

'Nomi, help Devorah put the coins in the charity box,' said Mama, and Nomi bent down to hoist up her little sister.

'Oof,' she exclaimed, 'you're getting so big and heavy!'

'Nomi,' squawked Esther, 'don't say that!'

Nomi blinked, bewildered, then she realised – of course, it encouraged bad luck to talk about a child being healthy.

'Sorry,' she whispered, and Esther gave three spits at the air to ward off the evil eye.

Then Mama draped her white lace shawl over her wig and held up her matchbox. 'Next week, God willing, my first daughter will light her own candles,' she said, and her voice trembled with emotion.

Nomi felt like crying again. The house would feel very strange without Adina in it. Then Mama struck the match, and Nomi hastily swallowed back her tears. On Shabbes, no one was allowed to be sad.

Indeed, that Friday night seemed to be the most joyous Nomi could remember. When Papa, her brothers, Peretz, Itsek, and two visitors came back from the Prayer House, they stamped and clapped

and roared the song of praise louder than ever
before:

'*An accomplished woman, who can find?*' they sang.
'*Her value is far beyond pearls.*'

Mama fingered her pearl necklace, beaming at
them.

'*Her husband's heart relies on her and he shall lack
no fortune.*

*She does him good, not evil, all the days of her life ...*'

Nomi glanced at Adina. She was standing very
straight and proud, her face lit up as if a lamp was
shining from inside it.

At dinner and all through the next day, everyone
seemed in a fever of happiness. On Shabbes afternoon
when Aaron and Yochevet arrived for lunch, the
whole family hauled them up the stairs to view the
new apartment.

'Look at this, look over here!' they all crowed.

As soon as lunch was over, Yochevet was pulled
by her excited sisters-in-law into their bedrooms to
view their new clothes.

And at the end of the day, when the Havdalah
candle was doused, while everyone was smearing
their eyelids with wine and wishing each other 'Good
week', Mama threw her arms around Adina.

'Oh, my daughter,' she warbled, 'this is your
wedding week!'

All the other children grabbed their sister too, in a huge, tight hug.

'Have a good week, Adina,' they shouted fervently.

At that moment, there was a knock at the front door. Who could be visiting now, at the end of Shabbes?

Shlomo ran to let them in, and the next instant there was the trill of a fiddle in the front hall, and a trio of klezmer musicians capered into the dining room.

'Good week!' they cried. 'A wedding week! Mazel tov! Congratulations!'

As they erupted into song, Mama hustled her girls into the kitchen and seized Adina by the hands.

'Dance!' she cried.

Miriam, Esther, Nomi and Devorah joined in, Bluma swaying in Esther's arms. Round and round they whirled, laughing and crying, while in the room next door the double bass throbbed, the flute twittered, the fiddle trilled, and the men sang.

## Chapter 19

# The Haircut

SUNDAY WHIRLED BY IN A blaze of activity. The girls twisted each other's hair into tight braids to set in waves for the wedding, and rushed in and out of each other's rooms to check on clothes, bags and hair ribbons. Mama kept darting off to the reception hall to make sure the huge cauldrons of fish and chicken were being cooked, while Yakov just ran around getting under everyone's feet.

Then, suddenly, it was Monday, the day before the wedding, and time to prepare the bride for the ceremony. At nightfall, a crowd of well-wishers were coming to escort Adina to her first bath at the mikve. Afterwards they would cram into the salon to witness the cutting of her hair and see her put on her marriage wig.

'Shlomo,' cried Mama, 'go tell Chaim we need to move the furniture in the salon. Nomi, run buy some oranges. Here, take my purse. Yakov, I told you not to touch those chocolates. Adina, is that cake ready for the oven? Miriam, don't take the glasses in yet; we need to move the furniture first. Oy, where's Chaim?'

When the old manservant appeared at last, the children excitedly helped him lift up the ebony table and chairs and move them to the side of the room. Esther spread a dark green velvet cloth on the table (slightly scratched from the betrothal party) and straightened up the bobbles round the edge of it. Miriam and Nomi covered the green rug with a large white sheet, patting it down so no one would trip. Then Miriam, Esther, Shlomo, Nomi, Yakov and Devorah picked up an armchair, all struggling and laughing to hold a part of it, and placed it in the middle of the sheet. This would be the hair-cutting chair.

'Mama, it's ready,' they called, racing back to the kitchen.

'Take in the food and plates then,' said Mama.

'I'm carrying the chocolates,' whooped Yakov.

Esther picked up the honey cake, fresh out of the oven, Miriam took the tray of glasses, Devorah took a bowl of nuts, Shlomo carried the orange slices, and Nomi brought up the rear with a stack of plates.

Chattering happily, they arranged everything on the table. Miriam took the soda syphon out of one of the glass-fronted cabinets, and Nomi ran to fetch more plates.

But in the kitchen doorway, she jerked to a halt. The bride-to-be was slumped over the table in a flood of tears, and Mama was standing over her, stroking her head.

'My ha-air,' wailed Adina.

'It will be all right, my precious daughter, I promise you it will be all right,' soothed Mrs Rabinovitch, but her voice shook, and she dabbed at her own eyes.

Nomi snatched up the plates and pelted back to the salon.

'Adina's bawling!' she announced.

'Huh, she's finally realised it's stupid to marry someone she's never met!' snorted Miriam.

'No, she's upset about getting her hair cut,' Nomi corrected.

She looked at the armchair, all by itself in the middle of the room, and imagined Adina sitting on it, with someone chopping off her beautiful long locks. It would be that very religious old woman who did it, the one who came to the shtibel on Holy Days, and told all the other women how to pray. Pious Zelda, they called her.

'Esther,' asked Nomi worriedly, 'Adina will look all right, won't she, with a wig on?'

'Of course she will,' said Esther.

Miriam pursed her lips.

That evening, dinner was barely over when the front hall began to fill with visitors – the women had arrived to escort the Rabbi's daughter to her first mikve. The family could hear their high-pitched voices laughing and chattering.

As soon as Papa finished grace, Mama pushed back her chair. 'Come, Adina,' she said. 'It is time to go.'

Nomi watched Adina rise reluctantly to her feet. She wanted to throw her arms around her big sister, hug her tight, and comfort her.

Devorah started to run after them, but Esther pulled her back. 'Not you, miss,' she said. 'It is only for older women. You and Bluma are off to bed now.'

Nomi and Miriam didn't talk much as they stood side by side washing the dinner dishes. Nomi tried to picture what was happening at the mikve.

'Does … does Adina have to get undressed with all those ladies watching her?' she whispered.

'I don't know,' growled Miriam. 'I guess so.'

Nomi felt her own cheeks burn with embarrassment at the thought of it.

They finished the dishes and went back to the dining room, where Esther was drawing with her pencils. At the other end of the table, Papa, Aaron and Shlomo pored over a book, pointing at words and arguing, while Yakov was sprawled across the table trying to build a tower from a pack of cards.

'Nomi, help me,' he called.

Nomi shook her head. She felt too nervous and churned up to balance flimsy cards on top of each other.

Sitting next to Esther, she rested her elbow on the table, put her chin on her hand, and stared at the clock on the mantelpiece.

To her left, Esther scratched away busily at her drawing, and on her other side, Yakov finished building his tower, puffed out his cheeks and blew it down.

She sighed, shifted to her other elbow, and waited. How long would it be till Adina came home?

At last there was the sound of voices on the stairs. All the girls leapt to their feet, and raced for the front hall.

A noisy mob of women poured in through the brown front door. Nomi jumped up and down trying to see Adina in the midst of them.

She caught a glimpse of her – just a white, terrified

face – and then she was swallowed up by the crowd again, and carried into the salon.

'Can we go in too?' demanded Nomi.

Miriam stuck out her chin. 'Well, *I* am,' she announced.

'Wait for me,' cried Nomi, but Miriam had already vanished.

Taking a deep breath, Nomi plunged in after her, worming her way among the pudgy, silk-clad bodies. She was almost suffocated by the smells of perfume and sweat, but she pushed her way through and burst out, gasping for air.

And there in front of her was the bride. Adina was huddled in the armchair, her hands over her face, while old Pious Zelda leaned over her, cackling and muttering, and snipping at her hair with a giant pair of shears.

Nomi stood there, frozen in dismay, as lock after lock of beautiful chestnut hair dropped to the floor.

Then the old woman straightened up and waved her scissors in the air.

'Done!' she announced, but before Adina could drop her hands, Pious Zelda jammed a cloth over her head.

'Shaving money before you look!' she cried, and began to move around the room, rattling a tin. 'Shaving money, shaving money,' she cackled.

There was laughter and joking as everyone dropped a few groshen into her tin.

At last the old woman made her way back to the armchair and laid a hand on Adina's head. 'Now you can see,' she said, and she whisked off the cloth.

Nomi gasped. The girl sitting on the chair did not look anything like her big sister. She had tiny curls all over her head, and now, with all that long hair gone, her eyes looked enormous, her eyebrows dark and sweeping, and her lips crimson.

'Mazel tov!' shouted the roomful of women.

But Adina clapped her hands over her head and looked up pleadingly at her mother.

'Wait, the wig!' cried Mrs Rabinovitch, waving her handkerchief in the air.

As eager hands seized the wig box from its perch on a china cabinet and passed it through the crowd, Nomi tapped her sister's knee. 'Adina,' she cried, 'you look beautiful just like that!'

Adina stared at her.

'Really?' she breathed.

'Really,' said Nomi emphatically.

The wig box reached Mama's hands and she wrenched it open.

'There, *now* look at her!' she said, thrusting a dark wig onto Adina's head.

Nomi's jaw dropped. The wig was cut in a short bob – the same style as the girls in Sura's fashion magazine.

'Aah! So chic! So up-to-date!' cried everyone in the room. Even Miriam stopped scowling and raised her eyebrows admiringly.

Adina looked anxiously at her younger sister. 'Nomi,' she asked, 'is it all right?'

Nomi felt embarrassed as all the women around turned to listen to her answer.

'Yes!' she breathed. 'You look like a bride in a fashion magazine!'

## Chapter 20

# Mordechai Arrives

And then, at last, it was the day of the wedding.

Squeaking with excitement, the girls followed Adina and Mama as they carried the wedding dress into the salon.

'We are dressing the bri-ide, we are dressing the bri-ide,' chanted Devorah.

Nomi closed the doors at both ends of the salon so none of the men would come in by mistake, and Adina pulled off her housedress. Underneath she was wearing one of the silk petticoats from her trousseau.

'O-oh,' breathed her sisters and her sister-in-law.

Every edge was hand-stitched into scallops, and embroidered with flowers.

Adina dragged off her thick cotton stockings and dropped them on the floor beside her housedress.

Then she perched on the yellow satin couch, and Yochevet handed her a small parcel done up in brown paper.

'These were the nicest ones I could find,' she said.

Adina peeled off the wrapping.

'O-oh!' cried everyone again as the silkiest, whitest pair of stockings slithered out.

'Well done, Yochevet,' said Mama.

A little chubby hand reached over to grab them.

'No, Bluma!' screeched Adina.

The baby had hoisted herself up on the edge of the couch.

'Esther, pick her up,' ordered Mama.

'Careful, she'll mess up your bow,' warned Adina.

On their heads, each of the sisters wore a giant taffeta bow the same colour as her dress. Miriam's was sky blue, Esther's pale yellow, Nomi's a soft sea green, and Devorah's pink.

'I'll take her,' said Miriam, holding out her arms. 'I look a clown anyway.'

'Don't talk nonsense, Miriam,' said Mama.

But nobody else argued. Nomi and Esther's hair was set in pretty rippling waves, while the plaits

Miriam had been wearing for the past two days had only made her hair stick out worse than usual.

Adina pulled on the new stockings, slid her feet into her shiny white wedding pumps, and stood up.

There was a tense pause as Mama slipped the wedding dress over her head, then...

'Oh,' breathed Nomi for the third time.

'It's gorgeous,' said Yochevet.

'Perfect,' nodded Esther.

'Like a princess,' said Devorah.

Sura had made the skirt in layers so that it fell below Adina's hips like the petals of a flower. As she turned slowly, the delicate white fabric fluttered and danced.

At that moment, there was a tap at the door.

'We're leaving for the station!' called Aaron.

Everyone in the room let out a scream. The men were going to fetch Mordechai Weinberg and his family!

Nomi, Esther and Yochevet raced for the balcony and squeezed together through the French windows to look down on the street below.

They saw a sea of men in black hats ebbing and flowing around a pair of droshkies drawn up at the kerb. A roar went up as Papa, Aaron, Shlomo, and Yakov came out through the gate. For an instant the Rabbi and his sons were swallowed in the crowd and then they appeared again, clambering into the droshkies.

Papa wore his antique girdle made of silver and studded with gemstones. It glittered and flashed as the Rabbi took his seat in the carriage. The three girls gazed at him with awe. On his head, despite the heat, he wore his best fur shtreimel.

'*Vyo, vyo!*' shouted the wagon drivers, flicking their reins.

And with a jangle of harness bells, the procession moved off, the droshkies in front and the crowd behind, cheering and singing.

'They're going to meet Mordechai! They're going to meet Mordechai!' shrieked Esther and Yochevet, jumping up and down and hugging each other.

As the older girls disappeared inside again, Nomi hung over the railing and watched the men out of sight.

'Please let Mordechai Weinberg be nice,' she prayed. 'Make Adina like him.'

Far in the distance, a tiny figure turned from the second wagon and waved to her. It was Yakov.

Then another carriage came bowling down the road and came to a halt.

'The bridal carriage!' gasped Nomi, and flung herself into the salon. 'Hey, everyone, our carriage is here!'

Then she stopped, gazing in awe.

Adina was wearing her veil. The soft lace seemed to float like a cloud of mist from the silver band around her head.

Mrs Rabinovitch stood back to look at her with tears rolling down her cheeks, but at the sound of Nomi's words she threw up her arms.

'Time to go,' she exclaimed.

The girls flew to snatch up their bags and check their own appearances in the mirror on the wall.

'Come on, come on, Adina,' they cried.

As they opened the door, Lidia came hurrying in from the other apartment.

'Oh, oh, I can't believe this is my little Adina!' she exclaimed.

A bunch of excited neighbours hovered at the foot of the stairs to wave them off.

'Mazel tov!' called Raisel the beggarwoman, lifting her toddler to see.

'Good luck!' quavered Old Chaim.

Nomi straightened her shoulders and smiled, feeling like a princess.

Zelig had drawn back both of the heavy, wrought-iron double gates, so the carriage stood framed by the tall archway. It was much bigger than an ordinary open-topped droshky. The sides were glossy black, and the four grey horses hitched to the front had white plumes bobbing on their heads.

The coachman jumped down to help Mama on board but she drew sharply back. A religious woman could not be touched by any man except her husband or son.

'Nomi,' she ordered, 'give me your hand.'

Once Mama and Adina were seated, the others clambered up the tiny steps. They piled onto the seat behind the driver, facing backwards.

'Everyone ready?' bellowed the coachman, and cracked his whip.

Nomi clutched her stomach. They were off to the wedding, off to meet Mordechai!

On the seat opposite, Mama sat very upright, looking grand and regal in her dress of deep blue satin, but Adina was hunched over, her eyes on something in her lap. It was a little prayer book, the one that Mordechai had sent her for a gift. Adina held it open, and her lips moved as she traced the words with her finger. Nomi looked at her anxiously. What was she thinking? What was she feeling?

When they drew up at the reception hall, the carriage was mobbed by the swarm of guests waiting outside.

'Ach, such a beautiful bride!' they cried as Adina stepped down, looking very pale.

Inside the reception hall, a strange-looking fellow

came capering towards them. He was dressed in wine-coloured knee breeches, grey stockings, a green waistcoat and a brown frockcoat.

'Welcome,' he chirruped, 'I am Benesh the Badchen.'

Nomi heaved a sigh. There was always a badchen at a wedding. He ran the occasion, telling everyone what to do, and making them laugh or cry with his lectures and comic poems. Usually, Nomi found the jokes embarrassing.

Benesh swept a bow so low his pointy little beard almost touched the floor, then he straightened up, gave an exaggerated start, and leapt backwards.

'*Oy vay*, what has happened to the bride?' he exclaimed.

'What?' cried her family, crowding around. Adina looked terrified.

'Tee hee!' chortled the badchen. 'Just joking. Naturally, the bride is perfect.'

Miriam and Yochevet snorted with laughter, and even Mama smiled, but Nomi clenched her fists and wished there didn't have to be a badchen.

'Come,' said Benesh, 'this is the banquet hall for the women.' He threw open a door, and ushered them in. 'Come, bride, and await your doom...tee hee, I mean your groom!'

Most of the room was filled with long, white-clothed tables, decorated with vases of scarlet dahlias. In a cleared space in front, a high-backed chair was draped in filmy white muslin and vines of purple clematis.

'Your throne,' declared the badchen with a bow.

As Adina took her seat, women from outside came pouring in.

The badchen let out a loud, startling, '*Aiiieeee!*' In a corner of the room, Shpilfogel the Fiddler and his klezmer band struck up a mournful tune.

Benesh began to sing.

'*Aiiee, weep, bride, weep,*' he keened, '*for today your old life ends.*

*Aiee, bride, weep, for today you leave the shelter and the care of your parents.*'

Adina and Mama began to dab at their eyes, and Nomi's throat tightened.

'*Aiee, bride, weep for the passing of your youth,*' the badchen went on.

'*Aiee, bride, weep and ask forgiveness for your sins.*'

Tears spilled down Nomi's cheeks, and everyone else in the room began to cry too.

Then, suddenly, there were cheers from outside.

Adina's head shot up. Two pink spots of excitement appeared on her cheeks. Nomi felt her own tears dry instantly.

'The groom has arrived!' cried Benesh.

There was a flurry in the doorway, and screeches

of, 'Mazel tov! Show us the bride!' and Mordechai's mother and aunts came rushing in.

They were dressed in clashing coral reds, lime greens and brilliant blues. Nomi felt as if a flock of parrots was descending on them as the women arrived at the chair, pecking on cheeks, flapping and squawking.

The room grew noisy with chatter and excitement. Mama and Mrs Weinberg began to dance, and the other women joined in, linking arms and whirling about. Baby Bluma was passed from hand to hand, pink-cheeked and laughing, but Adina, trapped in her chair, reached out to catch hold of her other sisters' hands and pull them close.

'Don't worry, Adina, we won't leave you,' said Nomi.

Devorah leaned against her sister's knee and Esther grasped her other hand, while Miriam reached out to grab a pastry from a passing waiter.

'Miriam, that's not very thoughtful,' said Nomi. She glanced at Adina. 'Are you starving?' she asked, for the bride and groom were not allowed to eat on their wedding day.

But Adina didn't answer. Her eyes had suddenly widened in terror. From outside in the hall came a surge of men's voices.

Nomi spun around to look.

There, in the doorway, stood Mordechai Weinberg.

His beard was as fiery-red as Yakov had described it, but Yakov had not mentioned his eyes. They were the blue of forget-me-nots, and they blazed now across the room towards his bride.

Nomi turned excitedly to her big sister, and saw, to her dismay, that Adina was sitting with her eyes glued to her prayer book again, not looking at Mordechai.

'Adina, *look!*' she squealed, shaking her sister's hand.

But Adina just blushed, and shook her head.

Mordechai took a step forward, and a crowd of men poured in around him, singing and rejoicing.

'*Siman tov u'mazel tov!*' they bellowed.

Nomi saw Papa and Reb Weinberg in the crowd, and Aaron and Shlomo and Yakov, and several boys with red hair who must be Mordechai's brothers.

They advanced across the room to Adina's chair, and then they drew to a halt and Mordechai stood there, staring down at his bride.

Now he was closer, Nomi could see tiny freckles all over his face, and bright, golden hairs mixed into his carroty beard.

'Don't stare,' hissed Esther.

Quickly, Nomi ducked her head, and slid her gaze sideways to Adina. She still wasn't looking!

Benesh began to sing again, and this time his only accompaniment was the sad twanging of Shpilfogel's violin.

'*Bride and groom, relatives, and friends,*' he warbled.
'*Hear what the badchen has to say!*
*Here sits the bride, as pretty as day,*
*But what does the fiddler have to say?*
*Beauty is fine, but it fades away!*'

As the violin went on wailing, Benesh thrust a basket towards the groom. Inside it lay a white headscarf made of silk.

'Bridegroom, veil your bride and show the world it is not her outward beauty you admire, but her inner soul.'

Mordechai lifted out the kerchief, fumbled, dropped it on the floor and knelt to pick it up. There were hisses of indrawn breaths all around the room.

But as the groom crouched on the floor, Nomi saw him tilt his face to look at his bride, and she saw Adina's eyelids flicker upwards. Just for an instant, the two of them gazed at each other.

The corners of Adina's mouth began to curl, and Mordechai's face lit in a relieved grin.

They like each other, thought Nomi, and she felt as if a tight band around her chest had snapped free.

Still smiling, Mordechai bounded to his feet, and draped the silken scarf over his bride's face.

He dropped it on purpose, Nomi realised.

## Chapter 21

# The Chuppah

'AND NOW FOR THE CHUPPAH,' proclaimed the man in purple pants.

Yakov let out a cheer and sprinted for the door. 'I get to help,' he yelled. 'She's my sister!'

He could hear the other boys pounding along behind him.

Bursting into the courtyard, he dived at the stack of long wooden poles decorated with ribbons.

'Hey!' he protested, as someone grabbed the other end of his pole. It was Mordechai's youngest brother, Michael.

Yakov tried to jerk it out of the six-year-old's hands, but the little carrot-top hung on fiercely.

'*Mine*,' he screeched.

Yakov looked around, but of course all the poles were taken now. Shlomo had one of them, and Mordechai's other brothers were already carrying the last two to the middle of the courtyard.

Yakov yanked angrily again. 'I got this first,' he growled.

'Michael, go pester one of your brothers,' said Aaron, arriving beside them. 'That's Yakov's pole.'

Triumphantly, Yakov jerked the stick upright.

'Hey, don't poke my eye out!' warned Aaron.

The sticks formed the posts of a square in the middle of the yard. Michael tried to snatch at his brothers', but they pushed him away. He turned to Yakov and poked out his tongue.

Yakov made a face back.

'Keep still,' ordered Aaron. He was trying to drape a large white prayer shawl over the top.

Yakov straightened up quickly and held his post as tightly as he could.

Meanwhile, the wedding guests were pouring in around them. The men filled up one side of the courtyard, the women and girls the other. The Rabinovitch sisters waited in a jiggling, impatient row in front of the women.

Yakov caught Nomi's eye and tilted his head proudly at the pole he was holding. Nomi nodded, and grinned back.

'There,' said Aaron, stepping away. 'The chuppah's ready.'

Above the four decorated poles, the shawl, with its tassels and gold embroidery, was stretched out to form a canopy.

At that moment, with a loud, penetrating wail, the badchen broke into a keening song that sent a shiver down Yakov's spine, but then there was the blare of a trumpet, and a troupe of musicians came marching down the aisle between the men and women.

Behind them strode Mordechai. He had put on a long white kittel over his black coat, and a fur shtreimel as big as Papa's on his head. His father and Papa Rabinovitch walked on either side of him, and everyone craned forward to see them.

'Papa!' squeaked Baby Bluma.

Her sisters giggled and shushed her.

As the three men stepped under the chuppah, the music quieted. Papa gestured to the prayer shawl above their heads.

'Mordechai,' he said, 'this represents the roof of your home. And now...your bride will enter your home for the first time!'

All eyes turned to the bride waiting in the doorway.

She looked like a statue, completely white from head to toe, the kerchief still draped over her face.

Mama stood to one side of her, and Mrs Weinberg on the other. Each of the older women held a burning candle in her hands.

Slowly, they began to move. The candles flickered, and Adina clung to the two mothers' arms. The crowd was silent – even Bluma, who stared with wide, solemn eyes.

Closer and closer they came, and then they reached the chuppah and began to circle around the groom.

The only sound was the *swish, swish, swish* of the women's skirts.

'One ...' counted Yakov. 'Two ...'

He knew Adina had to walk around Mordechai seven times. Aaron had whispered to him that the devil and his wife always hid, invisible, among the wedding guests, waiting to bring harm to a new husband and wife. The only way to escape was for the bride to weave a wall of protection by walking seven times around her groom.

'It has to be exactly seven,' Aaron had hissed, 'for seven is the number of the days of Creation.'

'Five ... six ...' counted Yakov. 'Seven!'

He heaved a little sigh of disappointment as

Adina took her place – safely – at the groom's side.
It would have been interesting to see what happened
if she got it wrong.

'*Baruch ata...*' rang out the voice of Papa. Today,
he was both the rabbi and the father of the bride.

He held the goblet of ruby-coloured wine high
in the air, sang the blessings, and took a sip. Now
it was the turn of the bride and groom. Mordechai
drank first, then Mama raised the covering from
Adina's face just enough to hold the wine glass to
her lips, and lowered it again.

'The ring,' beamed Papa.

Mordechai's brothers glanced over their shoulders.
'Michael,' they prompted.

With a triumphant smirk, Michael drew the ring
from his pocket, and gave it to his eldest brother.

'Adina, hold out your right hand,' said Papa.

Trembling, Mordechai placed the ring on the tip
of his bride's finger.

'*Haray at mekudeshet...*' he said, in a low voice.
'Behold, with this ring you are sanctified to me
according to the Law of Moses and Israel.' He slid
the ring down her slim white index finger.

Then Papa held up a scroll of parchment and
began to read out loud. It was the marriage contract,
but it was written in an old-fashioned language
Yakov could not understand.

He shuffled his feet and sniffed at the cooking smells wafting from the hall. Then he wiggled his shoulders and his fingers. His arms were getting stiff from keeping still so long.

'Careful,' growled Aaron, reaching up to hold the pole steady.

Papa put down the parchment, picked up the wine glass again, and began the seven blessings. When he reached the last one everyone joined in:

'Blessed are You Hashem our God, King of the universe, Who created joy and gladness, groom and bride...the sound of joyous wedding celebrations, the sound of young people feasting and singing...'

The words grew louder and louder. The ceremony was coming to an end.

Once again, the bride and groom were given the glass of wine, but this time they finished it off.

Solemnly, Papa wrapped the empty glass in a large white napkin, bent down, and placed it on the ground beside the groom.

There was a hush of expectation.

Mordechai lifted his foot.

*SMASH!* With one hard stomp, he crushed the bundle.

'Mazel tov!' shouted everyone.

Adina tore the covering from her face and, for one ecstatic moment, the bride and groom looked at each other with beaming smiles spreading across their faces.

But then, before they could exchange a word, their families came pouring over them with hugs and kisses, and the men exploded into song.

'*Chussen, kalleh, mazel tov!*' they sang. '*Groom and bride, good luck!*'

The joyful singing filled the courtyard and seemed to rise right up to heaven.

## Chapter 22

## Celebrations

NOMI GRABBED HER SISTER IN a tight hug.

'Happy?' she shouted in Adina's ear.

'Yes, of course,' cried the new bride, laughing as her sisters and sister-in-law all caught hold of her, embracing her and kissing her on the cheeks.

Every woman in the courtyard was pushing forward now, trying to reach the bride and wish her mazel tov, but Mama took hold of Adina's arm.

'Adina has to break her fast,' she cried. 'Let her through!'

'Let the bride through, let the bride through,' chanted the excited mob.

Laughing and hanging on to each other, the girls found themselves swept towards the hall. Ahead of them, Nomi could see the groom's white kittel and high fur shtreimel bobbing like a boat among the sea of men.

They poured into the foyer, and there was the badchen, standing by a side door, calling and beckoning.

'Make way for the bride and groom!' he called. 'Make way, make way.'

Mordechai erupted from the crowd of men and stumbled, breathless, towards the door, his shtreimel knocked sideways on his head. He grinned as Adina joined him.

The badchen bowed.

'Please enter,' he said.

Nomi and her sisters craned forward to see through the door as Adina and Mordechai slipped inside. It was a small room. In the centre, a table was spread with a white cloth, and two chairs stood facing the door.

Mordechai grasped the back of one chair to pull it out, and Adina took the seat, looking pink and flustered.

'Bring the golden soup!' called Benesh, and everyone turned to see a waiter coming through the crowd with a bowl on a tray.

As he passed, Nomi caught a glimpse of a golden-coloured broth glistening with chicken fat.

'They have to share it,' whispered Yochevet. 'Watch.'

Sure enough, the bride and groom each picked up a spoon as the waiter set down the bowl between them.

Yochevet giggled. 'At my wedding, some of the soup dribbled down my chin.' She gave a peal of laughter.

Esther and Nomi glanced at each other in horror. If Adina spilled soup down her chin she would be mortified. She would never laugh about it like Yochevet.

'Adina won't spill any soup!' declared Devorah confidently, and the others grinned. The little girl was right.

The waiter came out again, and Benesh pulled the door shut and turned to the crowd.

'Go, go,' he ordered. 'Now is the time for feasting and rejoicing. The bride and groom will join you shortly.'

With a roar of approval, the guests streamed towards the banquet rooms, the men to one room, the women to the other.

'Food!' whooped Miriam. 'Come on.'

As the others hurried after Miriam, Nomi stood

staring at the closed door, wondering what was happening behind it. Were Adina and Mordechai talking to each other, or were they too shy?

'Hey, Nomi!' Yakov suddenly bobbed up beside her, tugging her sleeve. 'Papa says to come and help.' He pulled her towards the men's banquet room. 'In here.'

'But...'

Nomi halted in the doorway. Men were milling everywhere, some of them crowded around the hand-washing basins at the side of the room, and others making their way towards the long, white-draped tables.

'Hurry and wash your hands,' said Yakov.

'But...what does Papa want me to do?' asked Nomi.

'Sssh,' hissed Yakov, and pointed.

At the table of honour, the Rabbi was waiting to recite a blessing. He had his hands poised over the biggest challah Nomi had ever seen. The loaf was almost as long as the table.

Yakov dived into the crowd to reach the hand-washing station but Nomi hung back, embarrassed by the men towering and jostling around her.

Only when the men were finished did she reach for a jug. Hastily, she mumbled her prayer, and turned, feeling conspicuous in her pale green dress in this room full of black-clad men.

'*Baruch ata ...*' intoned Papa.

Beside him was an empty seat for the groom, and on the other side of that sat chubby Reb Weinberg, beaming around the room. The brothers of the groom and bride filled the other seats.

The prayer came to an end, and with a loud 'Amen', the guests attacked the fresh rolls and jugs of wine on the tables in front of them. Waiters came pouring out of the kitchen with trays of gefilte fish, and Nomi threaded her way towards her father.

He was slicing up the huge loaf of challah and piling it onto platters.

'Ah, Nomi,' he said. 'We need to serve these gentlemen.'

He nodded at two tables near him and Nomi saw they were filled with beggars. She recognised Little Nussyn and Big Nussyn, and Wulf with his missing leg, and all the other men from Thursday afternoons. They were dressed in their usual tattered clothes, ill-fitting, stained and tied up with bits of string, and they looked as out of place as Nomi felt herself. But a wedding was only truly blessed if poor people were invited, and they had to be served by the host's own hands (or the hands of his family).

'Your health, Rabbi!' '*L'chaim!*' 'Long life!' shouted the beggars, clinking glasses and tossing wine down their throats.

'Happiness from your children,' bellowed Little Nussyn.

'And even greater wealth!' yelled someone else, and they all chuckled.

'And health to you, brothers,' the Rabbi responded. 'Drink hearty. Long life.'

He picked up a platter of bread and Nomi did the same.

'No, Nomi. You go fetch the fish from the kitchen,' said Papa. 'I will serve the bread.'

Nomi looked at the door to the kitchen. It kept banging open as each new waiter came barging out with a heavy load balanced on his fingers. Sucking in her breath, she ducked inside.

The kitchen was a shock of noise and heat and flame.

Cauldrons bubbled over open fires. Cooks in long white aprons stirred and yelled, while waiters with perspiring faces grabbed dishes, and yelled back. In the midst of it all, Mama, in her dark blue satin and diamonds, prodded at a huge roast goose that had just been pulled from the oven, steaming and sizzling in its dish.

'Make sure you give the best portions to the groom's family,' she shouted to a waiter over the racket. 'God forbid they should be offended!'

She spotted Nomi, and pointed at a tray on a table.

'That is the fish for the beggars,' she called.

Nomi heaved up the tray, but as she took a few nervous steps towards the banquet room, the door flew open and a waiter came crashing through.

'Hey!' he snarled, swerving around her.

Trembling, Nomi waited while he snatched up another platter of food, then she quickly slid out after him.

The first thing she noticed was Mordechai, sitting in his place at the table of honour. He and Adina must have finished their soup.

As she walked past, he smiled and waved to her.

'Hello!' he called.

Nomi beamed back at him in surprise. There were not many young men who would notice a little girl, and say hello.

She walked on, a singing feeling in her heart. Adina had married a kind man.

She was still smiling as she set down the heavy tray on one of the beggars' tables.

'Mazel tov, Miss.' 'Thank you, Miss,' said the men.

She lifted a slice of fish, slid it onto the first plate, and looked down proudly. She had served it without spilling any of the stuffing.

But, 'Just shove it on, Miss. Never mind how it looks,' called Big Nussyn, and they all began to thrust their plates towards her.

'All tastes the same,' chuckled Little Nussyn.

In a fluster, Nomi began to tip the fish higgledy-piggledy onto their plates.

'That's the way, Miss.' 'Come on, Miss, we're hungry!' they encouraged her, grabbing their plates back and stuffing the food eagerly into their mouths.

Nomi began to giggle, pushing the fish off faster and faster. When she turned to the next table, she was almost overwhelmed by the barrage of plates.

'Here, Miss!' 'Don't forget me, Miss,' voices shouted at her.

On the stage, Shpilfogel's klezmer band was tuning up. The trumpet bleated and the strings twanged.

'Hurry, Miss!' 'We want to dance!' called the beggars.

'Nomi,' said Papa in her ear, and she spun round, embarrassed for him to see her serving so messily. He didn't seem to notice. 'When you finish serving this, you should go to the other room and eat. Shlomo and Aaron will help me with the next courses.'

Nomi had barely scraped the last slice onto a plate when the band struck up a dance tune. A surge of excitement pulsed through her arms and legs, but she had to watch enviously as all the men around her pushed back their chairs and rushed for the dance floor. She couldn't join in – it would not be seemly for a rabbi's ten-year-old daughter to dance with men.

As she made her way to the door, the mass of black-clad figures kicked and stamped across the bare patch of floorboards and burst over the edges, crashing into chairs and tables. She saw Papa and Mordechai leaping in a circle with the beggars, their arms entwined. She saw Yakov copying Aaron, kicking up his heels Cossack style, and Mordechai's little red-haired brother pushing him over, and all of them laughing.

Regretfully, she stepped out of the room.

And then she remembered that Adina would be waiting in the women's banquet hall. She could tell her big sister about Mordechai smiling at her, and about him dancing with the beggars. And maybe she could even find out what he had said to his new bride while they were eating their soup.

## Chapter 23

# The Last Dance

NOMI BURST INTO THE BANQUET hall, then stopped short, staring at her big sister. Adina looked so different!

It was that marriage wig, and the way she chatted with the older women, looking them straight in the eye instead of keeping her gaze cast down (the way she always told Nomi to do).

She isn't Adina Rabinovitch any more, realised Nomi with a pang. She is Mrs Mordechai Weinberg now.

She slid into her seat, feeling too shy to speak to this new, grown-up Adina.

'Nomi!' Devorah turned a food-smeared grin towards her, and waved something in the air. 'Eat this.' Before Nomi could stop her, the four-year-old was pushing a half-chewed chicken leg into her mouth.

'N-o-o, Devorah, that's yours!' laughed Nomi. 'Look, I've got my own.'

Wiping her cheek with her napkin, she glanced at her plate. It was heaped high with roast chicken, sweet-and-sour meatballs and sliced veal.

'Nomi,' called Mama over the little girl's head, 'you must taste everything.'

'Yes, Mama.'

They were seated at a long table, looking out over the sea of guests. In the centre, Adina held court like a queen, the row of Mordechai's relatives stretching to her left and the Rabinovitch family to her right (Mama first, then Devorah, Nomi, Miriam, and last of all Esther, with Bluma on her lap).

'Mmm, look,' breathed Miriam, as a waiter approached, bearing a whole roast goose on a tray.

This was a feast for a rabbi's daughter, and platter after platter appeared from the kitchen.

Each of the sisters had a favourite. Devorah's was the carrot tsimmes, hot and sticky with honey, Esther preferred the spicy dill pickles and the sauerkraut with berries, Nomi liked the kugel with the thick, fatty noodles, and Bluma loved anything she could squash between her fingers, especially the jellied calves' feet, cold and wobbly on her plate.

After a while, though, each of them (except for Miriam) began to flag. By the time the sweets arrived, Devorah could only take one lick of chocolate cake before she flopped against Nomi, her eyelids drooping. Bluma fell asleep on Esther's shoulder, and Nomi, feeling as full and puffed-up as one of the raisins in the compote, pushed her plate away. From the corner of her eye, she saw Adina do the same.

'No, don't stop,' wailed Mrs Rabinovitch.

Seizing a serving spoon, she piled up chocolate cake, lemon sponge, walnut tart and apple compote on Nomi and Adina's plates and pushed them back again. 'Eat, eat,' she commanded, then she jumped up and rushed around to make sure Mrs Weinberg was eating everything too.

Nomi stared at her plate. If she ate all this she would burst. She glanced sideways. The new bride flashed her a rueful grin, screwed up her face, and plunged a spoonful into her mouth as if she was taking a dose of castor oil. Chuckling, Nomi picked up her own spoon. Maybe Adina wasn't so grown-up after all!

Then suddenly Benesh the Badchen was back among them.

'It is time for the Mitzvah Dance!' he carolled. 'Bring the bride!'

'The Good Luck Dance,' shrieked Mama, leaping out of her chair.

'The Mitzvah Dance,' cried Mrs Weinberg.

Laughing and pushing Adina from behind, the two mothers hustled her towards the door.

Miriam and Esther jumped up to follow, Esther carrying Bluma in her arms.

'Devorah, wake up!' Nomi shook the little girl slumped against her shoulder. 'Come on, it's time to watch the Mitzvah Dance.'

The sleepy four-year-old stumbled off her chair, and Nomi hauled her out of the room.

In the foyer, Mama, Mrs Weinberg, Esther and Miriam were clustered at the entrance to the men's banquet hall, peering in.

'Miriam!' urged Nomi, tugging her sleeve.

Miriam stepped back, and Nomi and Devorah squeezed inside.

Adina stood alone, very small and white, in the centre of the dance floor, and as the band struck up a tune, Benesh the Badchen began to sing.

'*Brothers and brothers-in-law,*' he warbled, '*come and dance for your sister and bring her joy.*'

With one spring, Aaron was out of his seat and leaping towards Adina. Shlomo tried to rise too, but a look of astonishment crossed his face and he sat down abruptly. Nomi saw him push back the tablecloth and peer under it. The next instant, Yakov and the groom's little brother shot out from beneath like a pair of scurrying rats.

Nomi burst out laughing. Those two rascals must have tied Shlomo's shoelaces to the chair!

Aaron scooped up the end of the long silk sash dangling from Adina's wrist, and began to kick and cavort, while everyone cheered him on. He was weaving Adina all the joy he could, and she flashed him a grateful smile before she modestly bowed her head again.

Laughing and panting to a halt, Aaron passed the sash to Mordechai's middle brothers. The two redheads held it between them, and began a shuffling, embarrassed waddle.

'Fathers, your turn next,' called the badchen.

Round, jolly Reb Weinberg bounced up to Adina and trotted around her, flapping his end of the sash.

But when it was Papa's turn, he let the sash drop to the ground. After all, a father could hold his own daughter's hands.

The music slowed as Adina raised her head to look at him, and Papa gazed back, his eyes brimming with tenderness. Nomi knew he was murmuring a prayer for her happiness.

'And finally, the gentleman you have all been waiting for,' announced the badchen. 'Mordechai Weinberg, come and dance with your bride!'

Mordechai bounded from the edge of the dance floor and grasped hold of the sash, not at the far end like his brothers and father had done, but right up close, almost touching Adina's fingers.

For an instant, he and Adina stared at each other, and then they began to move, slowly at first, taking a step back, then coming together again, a step back, and together again, their eyes never leaving each other's faces.

A lump rose in Nomi's throat and she felt a hand grip her shoulder. It was Mama, laughing and crying as usual, and hugging everyone she could reach. Nomi grinned back through her own tears. Esther was gazing at the young couple with a blissful expression, while baby Bluma, awake again, was jigging happily, and even Miriam had a smile on her face.

Nomi glanced at Devorah, and the two of them squeezed hands, beaming at each other.

Then Mordechai let out a yell. 'Louder!' he shouted to the band. 'Faster!'

Flinging away the sash, he grasped hold of his bride. And the two figures, one tall and carrot-haired, one small and dark, exploded in a blur of dance, laughing and whirling, faster and faster.

Nomi heaved a contented sigh. Mordechai was kind and considerate and fun. He would make Adina a good husband. Papa and the matchmaker had chosen well.

# Author's Note

THIS BOOK IS BASED ON actual people and events. The 'Nomi' of the story was my Nana Nomi, and I developed the other characters – mischievous Yakov, rebellious Miriam, and so on – from Nana's descriptions of her real brothers and sisters. The scrapes and adventures they get up to in the story are based on truth. Adina, at the age of fifteen, really did get married to a boy she had never met!

Unfortunately, when the real Rabinovitch children grew up, they had to face the perils of the Second World War and the Holocaust. This was a time when the lives of Jewish people were threatened just because they were Jewish. Tragically, only Nomi, Esther and Miriam survived, but this book has been an attempt to bring the whole family back to life again and to help them live forever in the happy days of their childhood. I hope you have enjoyed getting to know them and becoming part of their lives.

Anna Ciddor, Melbourne, 2016

# Glossary

*NOTE ON YIDDISH AND HEBREW pronunciation: Hebrew and Yiddish words should be written with Hebrew letters. The versions here are common English transcriptions for the words used in this book. The 'ch' spelling represents a sound similar to 'h' but made in the back of the throat (except for the word 'chulent' where the 'ch' is pronounced in the usual English way). Yiddish speakers like the Rabinovitches usually put emphasis on the first syllable of a word.*

**Babka** (Yiddish) – A loaf made by rolling out dough, spreading it with a sweet filling, then rolling it up and adding a topping of sugar and cinnamon.

**Badchen** (Hebrew) – A master of ceremonies for a wedding. He runs the occasion, telling everyone what to do, and makes them laugh or cry with his lectures and comic poems.

**Bagel** – A doughnut-shaped bread roll that is boiled before it is baked.

**Bar Mitzvah** – This is when a Jewish boy turns thirteen and is considered to be spiritually mature. He now has the full rights and responsibilities of a Jewish man, such as the right to be called up to read from the Torah in a synagogue.

**Baruch ata** (Hebrew) – 'Blessed are you', the opening words of a prayer.

**Baruch ata Adonai Eloheinu melech ha'olam** (Hebrew) – 'Blessed are You, Adonai our God, Sovereign of the Universe', the opening words of a prayer.

**Beadle** – See *shammes*.

**Blacksmith** – A person who forges objects such as horseshoes out of iron, and puts shoes on horses.

**Calcimine** – An old-fashioned type of paint used for walls and ceilings.

**Castor oil** – An unpleasant-tasting vegetable oil given to children in the past as a remedy for various medical complaints.

**Challah** (Yiddish and Hebrew) – Bread traditionally used for *Shabbes*, made of a slightly sweet egg dough, and plaited.

**Chamber pot** – When people did not have toilets in their homes they often kept a pot under the bed to use at night.

**Chulent** (Yiddish) – A stew traditionally eaten in Jewish homes for Saturday lunch. The usual ingredients are meat, potatoes, barley and beans. The stew is cooked over a low heat from late on Friday until it is served.

**Chuppah** (Yiddish and Hebrew) – A canopy supported by four poles, which is suspended over the bride and groom during the Jewish wedding ceremony.

**Chussen** (Yiddish and Hebrew) – Bridegroom.

**Cobbler** – A person who makes or mends shoes.

**Compote** – Stewed fruit.

**Credenza** – A side cabinet, usually in a dining room.

**Dowry** – Money or property brought by a wife to her husband at the time of their marriage. A girl would spend her life filling her dowry chest until she got married.

**Droshky** – An open horse-drawn carriage with four wheels that was used in Poland and Russia.

**Dziękuję** (Polish) – 'Thank you' (pronounced 'jenkooyeh').

**Ebony** – A black-coloured wood obtained from a tropical tree and used for furniture.

**Eiderdown** – A feather-filled quilt.

**Gefilte fish** – A traditional Jewish dish made by mincing fish. Nowadays it is often served as balls of minced fish but 'gefilte' literally means 'stuffed' in Yiddish.

**Girdle** – A broad band worn around the waist.

**Goy** (Yiddish) – Non-Jew; can be used in a derogatory way.

**Groshen** (Yiddish) – Small coins.

**Ha'rei zo challah** (Hebrew) – 'This is Challah'. Although the whole loaf is referred to as the 'challah', the word challah actually means the piece of dough broken off and burnt. This piece symbolises the offerings that used to be made at the ancient Temple in Jerusalem. By making this offering, the baking of bread becomes a spiritual act.

**Havdalah** (Hebrew) – The religious ceremony marking the end of the Sabbath.

**Hebrew** – The language used in the Jewish Bible, and as a spoken language in Israel.

**Herring** – A type of fish, often served pickled in oil and salt.

**Ironmongery** – A shop that sells hardware.

**Kalleh** (Yiddish and Hebrew) – Bride.

**Kerchief** – A square headscarf.

**Kerosene** – A type of oil commonly used in lamps but also used as shampoo at this time.

**Kiddush** (Yiddish and Hebrew) – A word that refers to the blessing said over wine on the Sabbath and other Holy Days.

**Kittel** (Yiddish) – A white robe worn by Jewish men for their wedding, for special Holy Days and as a burial shroud.

**Klezmer** – Refers to a Jewish style of music from Eastern Europe, or the musicians who play that style of music.

**Klutz** (Yiddish) – A clumsy person.

**Kosher** - Food that complies with or is prepared according to Jewish dietary religious laws.

**Kugel** (Yiddish) – A baked pudding traditionally eaten in Jewish homes. Typical ingredients are egg noodles, chicken fat, sugar and raisins.

**L'chaim** (Hebrew) – A toast which means 'To life'.

**Linoleum** – A smooth, hard floor covering.

**Matchmaker** – A person who arranges a marriage by bringing two people together.

**Mazel tov** (Yiddish and Hebrew) – This phrase literally means 'good luck' but it is often used for 'Congratulations'.

**Melave Malka** (Yiddish and Hebrew) – This phrase literally means 'escorting the Queen', and refers to the meal at the end of the Sabbath (the Sabbath is often referred to as the 'Queen').

**Mikve** (Yiddish and Hebrew) – A bath used for ritual purification.

**Modah anee lefanecha** (Hebrew) – 'I give thanks to You', the first words of a prayer that is said on waking up in the morning to thank the Almighty for the gift of life. (A girl says 'Modah anee' and a boy says 'Modeh anee'.)

**Nu** (Yiddish) – 'So?' 'Well?'

**Pious** – Devoutly religious.

**Pound** – A non-metric unit of measurement. One pound is a bit less than half a kilogram.

**Proszę** (Polish) – 'Please', 'you're welcome', or 'here you are' (pronounced 'proshah').

**Przestańcie** (Polish) – 'Stop that' (pronounced 'pshe'stan'chi')

**Rabbi** – A spiritual leader of a Jewish community.

**Reb** (Yiddish) – Mister.

**Samovar** – An urn that heats water for making tea.

**Sauerkraut** – Shredded cabbage pickled in salt water.

**Shabbes** (Yiddish) – Sabbath.

**Shalom Aleichem** (Hebrew) – 'Peace be upon you', the opening words of a song traditionally sung by men returning home from the synagogue or *shtibel* on Friday night.

**Shammes** (Yiddish) – An official at a synagogue or *shtibel* who performs useful jobs.

**Shtibel** (Yiddish) – A place for prayer and for study of the Torah.

**Shtreimel** (Yiddish) – A large round fur hat made of animal tails worn on top of the skull cap on the Sabbath, Holy Days and special occasions.

**Siedzieć** (Polish) – 'Sit' (pronounced 'shyedyech').

**Skillet** – Frying pan.

**Soda syphon** – A bottle with a special attachment for making carbonated drinks.

**Taffeta** – A crisp, fine-quality fabric often made of silk.

**Talmud** – The collection of Jewish religious laws based on interpretations of the Bible by rabbis in ancient times.

**Torah** – The first five books of the Bible.

**Trousseau** – The new clothes made for a bride in time for her wedding, including her wedding gown and underwear.

**Tsimmes** (Yiddish) – A traditional Jewish stew in which the main ingredients are usually carrots and honey.

**Tsitsis** (Yiddish) – A ritual garment with tasselled fringes at each corner worn by religious Jewish males under their clothes as a constant reminder of religious obligations.

**Vyo** (Polish) – 'Giddy-up'.

**Yeshiva** – A secondary school where Jewish boys study the *Torah* and *Talmud*.

**Yid** – A slang word for Jew, usually used in a derogatory way.

**Yiddish** – A Jewish language that developed from High German, Hebrew and Slavic languages. It is written using Hebrew letters.

**Yom hashishi** (Hebrew) – 'The sixth day', the opening words of the *Kiddush*.

**Złoty** (Polish) – Polish currency (pronounced 'zwoteh').

# Acknowledgements

THE AUTHOR EXTENDS A HUGE 'THANK YOU' TO:

her late grandmother, whose inspiring and detailed reminiscences formed the basis for this book;

other precious people the author discovered who remember life in Poland before the War and helped fill in the gaps;

Rabbi Velly Slavin and his relatives around the world for replying so rapidly and unstintingly to questions about religion;

her sister Tamar for ever-faithful assistance in polishing the manuscript;

Magda Pokrzycka, who was a friend as well as a guide on the author's visit to Lublin;

Bartosz Gajdzik and his colleagues from the Grodzka Gate-NN Theatre Centre who painstakingly research and preserve Lublin's lost Jewish heritage;

the Jewish Research Institute who helped the author trace documents about her family's history;

Dr Luba Matraszek, and all the other amazing people in Lublin and Warsaw who embraced this project and went out of their way to assist the author, including the staff at the archives offices, the Jewish Historical Institute and the Polin Museum of the history of Polish Jews;

the team at Allen and Unwin for the love, respect and attention to detail they have poured into publishing this book; and

all the readers of the manuscript whose enthusiastic responses gave the author the encouragement to keep on working for four years.

# About the author

ANNA CIDDOR has written and illustrated fifty-six books on topics as diverse as Vikings, travel, Australian history, and goldfish. Whatever the topic, she hunts out every tiny detail so her readers can immerse themselves, as she does, in another world.

For *The Family with Two Front Doors* – the story of her Nana Nomi's childhood – Anna travelled across the world from her home in Melbourne, Australia, to Lublin, Poland, to do her research. She found the apartment block where the Rabinovitches lived, and as she entered through the black wrought-iron gates, she felt as if she was stepping back in time. She saw the staircase where Yakov clattered up and down, she found the courtyard where the children played among the washing lines, and she gazed up at the balcony, imagining Nomi and her sisters standing there at the end of the Sabbath watching for the first stars...

Anna's bestselling books have been translated into other languages, recorded as audio books and shortlisted for various awards. They have twice been selected as Notable Books by the Children's Book Council of Australia, and in 2005 Anna was awarded a grant by the Literature board of the Australia Council for the research and writing of *Night of the Fifth Moon*.

Find out more about Anna Ciddor, and her books at

**www.annaciddor.com**